To Ken —
Best of luck to
an ex team mate

Bill Virdon

"I am pleased and honored that Ken would ask me to be a part of the foreword of this book. I was a teammate of Ken's and have seen the results of his professional baseball scouting career. There is no one more qualified to entertain young readers on the subject of baseball."

Bill Virdon
Manager - Houston Astro's
Baseball Club

"Ken was a top scout in the Pittsburgh Pirate organization and was involved in the scouting and signing of many of our top players. He knows talent as well as anyone in baseball. He is not only capable of judging a potential Major League baseball prospect, but can teach and develope young players as well. Ken is a gentleman in every respect and it is our privilege to have been associated with him."

> Harding Peterson
> General Manager &
> Executive Vice President
> Pittsburgh Pirate
> Baseball Club

"Knowing Ken the past 20 years as one of the top Major League baseball scouts in the country, I find it very rewarding to be able to write a few words in his behalf. For some 12 years I have served as hitting coach at his many Youth Baseball Camps in Michigan and Indiana. The players he signed, and his great success as a player, certainly qualifies him as an expert on anything pertaining to young player development. I know by reading his books you will be impressed by his true love for our National Game."

> Charlie "Paw Paw" Maxwell
> Former Detroit Tiger Outfielder

"Ken Beardslee brings a truly unique background to his writing. His experience as a sandlot player, a high school star, a professional player and finally a top professional baseball scout, enables him to write with a base of knowledge possessed by few. His love for the game of baseball and feelings for those who play it will provide young players a rich reading experience."

Fred Decker
Head Baseball Coach
Western Michigan University

"It was a lucky day when Ken Beardslee started his baseball camp in Indiana. Ken brings a rich professional background to Hoosier baseball. His playing days with the Yankee organization and a long successful career as a major league scout with the Pittsburgh Pirates has allowed him to see and understand baseball from every level."

Bill Jones
Baseball Coach
DeKalb High School
1980 State Champs

"It has been my privilege to have known Ken Beardslee for approximately 15 years. In my opinion he is one of the top baseball scouts that I have known. Ken is one of the most honest and reliable people in his profession. He is highly intelligent and very articulate. There are not many people whose opinion I respect as much as Ken's when it comes to baseball."

Dave Alexander
Head Baseball Coach
Purdue University

CONTENTS

HOME IS WHERE YOU HANG YOUR SPIKES

Printed in the United States of America
Printed by Light and Life Press
Winona Lake, Indiana 46590

Ken/Mari Baseball Publications
Milford, Indiana 46542

For additional copies of this book
please write —
       Ken/Mari Baseball Publications
       Box 68, RR # 1
       Milford, Indiana 46542

Drawings and Cover
by Bev Beardslee

Books by Ken Beardslee

The Kid From Connersburg
Little Field On The Corner
Home is Where You Hang Your Spikes

CHAPTER
1
IN AND OUT OF RETIREMENT

Frank Knight decided the walk would do him good. Besides, no sense getting the little Plymouth out of the garage when the Burlington Baseball Club offices were only five blocks from his front porch. Outside the snow was falling faster, and the wind tore at his clothing. His overcoat was tight, and he turned the collar up so it nearly touched the brim of his grey felt hat. He turned off Henry Street and walked slowly past a row of large clapboard houses. The wide porches, without their wicker chairs, seemed cold and unfriendly as the wind swept across their bare floors.

He wondered why Harley Walsh, the Burlington Bears' owner, had insisted that he get over to the ball park. Last season the Bears had won their first pennant, and it had been his best year in professional baseball. As a scout for Harley, he had signed young Joel Travis, a right handed pitcher from Connersburg. The boy, only 18 years of age, had won nearly 20 games for Burlington. He had been far and away, the best sign of the year in the class "A" Central League.

Shortly after the close of the season, Frank had met with Harley and informed the owner that he was retiring. He was about to celebrate his 65th. birthday. It was time to hang up the uniform while he was on top. He had spent better than forty years in professional baseball; nearly 20 of those were in service to the Burlington ball club. Besides, Burlington had a veteran club returning, with one of the best managers in the business signed for the 1948 season. George Hauser was known as "The Wizard" of minor league skippers. Last season he had came up with a new infield alignment system for Joel Travis. The youngster, due to a severe physical disability, was unable to make the routine fielding plays off the mound. The new alignment had enabled Joel to pitch effectively against top minor league hitters. Frank chuckled to himself. Ole George hadn't been hiding behind the door when the smarts were being handed out.

When he walked into the main office, he noticed Greta Crim, Harley's secretary, filing some papers behind her desk.

"Hello Greta!" Frank sang out. "Where's the man with all the money?"

Greta scoffed, "You must be lost, Frank. No one with money around this place. If you doubt my word, I'll show you last week's pay stub."

Frank answered very solemnly. "Greta, I'm really sorry to hear you talk like that. Harley told me only last week that you were drawing one of the best pay checks on the club. You know Harley, Greta. His word has always been the gospel."

Greta slammed the filing drawer shut. "Frank, you might just as well go bother somebody else. I got up this morning feeling wonderful, and I plan to stay that way, no matter who walks in that door. Harley's in the other office, so why don't you scoot in there and rile him up? Just because you've been put out to pasture doesn't mean you have a license to come in here with all your nonsense. You and Harley — two of a kind. He's as tight as the mainspring on that wall clock. If he doesn't buy me some new equipment for this office, I'm going to bounce this old typewriter off his head."

Frank fought hard to hold back a laugh. He walked quickly toward Harley's office. He was smart enough to know when to make a fast exit.

Harley seemed pleased that he had dropped

everything and arrived at the park in a few short minutes.

"Frank, have a seat. Something mighty important has surfaced. Time for a meeting of the minds."

Frank's eyebrows went up.

The owner continued, "I've got to make an important decision within the next few days. I plan to talk with Hauser this afternoon. I want your opinion this morning." Harley took a rather deep breath and leaned forward in his chair. "Two gentlemen from the class "AA" Atlantic League visited me yesterday. Frank, they want us in their league this summer! Can you imagine such a thing? Burlington, with but 60,000 people, in a "AA" league! So help me, Frank, when those fellas told me their business, I nearly fell off this chair. They said they felt the Bears had the player personnel to compete in "AA" baseball. Apparently all the good publicity we received last fall was a factor in their selection. I'll tell you, Frank, I can see some great things happening if we make the move. Attendance is bound to improve with a better class of player competing in the stadium. There's just one hitch. I know, and you know, there is no way we can make that first division with our present roster. They may think so, but we know better. I've seen most of those clubs during the past year. Over 142 games they would bury us. All those dreams of better attendance would evaporate with a seventh or eighth place finish. In the class "A" Central League we have a chance to repeat as champions."

Frank nodded in agreement. "My first question would be what about Miller, Pearce, and Wilkins? These three players had great stats last season. It's nonsense to consider "AA" baseball without these guys on the roster. Wilkins and Pearce could make the difference between a first and second division finish. George told me that all three players were headed for higher baseball. Is that true?"

Harley nodded, "I can sell the contracts of all three to "AA" clubs. And that's exactly what I'll do if we stay in the Central League. But, if we decide to jump into the Atlantic League, I'll try to talk them into joining the club here. It's only a guess on my part, but I would say all three could be signed for Burlington without difficulty. Double A salaries are pretty much the same around the country."

"Well, Harley," Frank smiled broadly, "appears you have some deep thinking to do. That's one nice thing about this retirement stuff — sort of eliminates that type of headache. I was just telling Greta, —"

'Frank, I've been thinking about something else. Funny, you mentioned retirement. Not all it's cracked up to be, you know. Makes a fellow lazy, cantankerous, and sort of worthless, you might say. Now in your case — especially your case — I've noticed it's changed your whole personality. You used to be a very witty fellow; sharp as a tack you were. George used to remind me of that fact. Now that sharpness has a rather dull edge; you know what I'm trying to say Frank? It's a darn shame. I'd like to give you back your old job, but it's like an old horse put out to pasture. When he's brought back into the barn and fitted with harness, he's stale, big bellied, and like as not forgot everything he ever knew. Now George was telling me - - - -"

Frank eyed the owner sternly, "Harley, you can rant and rave all you like. You're not talking me out of retirement. I've bought enough fishing equipment to last me for twenty years, and, by George, I plan on putting it to good use. Now if you want my opinion on this Atlantic League business, here it is for what it's worth." Frank paused for a moment and then chosing his words carefully, remarked, "In my judgment the switch would be a great opportunity to upgrade baseball in this city. With another two good pitchers I believe the present staff could hold its own. If you can talk Miller, Wilkins, and Pearce into staying on, the infield is set. I would try to sign another good right hand hitting outfielder. You might also consider picking up a third string catcher. Joel will be reporting the middle part of May. The first

4

four or five weeks will be a good test for the pitching staff, but George will think of something to stay in contention. That's my honest opinion, Harley, and now, if you don't mind, I'm leaving for lunch.''

The owner threw up his hands in disgust. ''Never thought you would run out when the ball club needed your help, Frank. I'm in this business to serve the community. It's a nasty job at times, but someone has to carry the load. I guess I don't matter to a living soul except myself.''

Frank smiled, ''Won't work Harley. Those sad songs roll off me like rain off a turtle's back.'' Before departing the room, he offered, ''By the way. I believe Greta could use a new typewriter. I suggested a check of all the equipment in there. She probably has a list prepared that's longer than that face of yours!''

The owner's reply was very sweet. ''May your fishing boat spring a leak, Frank.''

The veteran scout laid aside baseball for the next three days. On Saturday Mary always went visiting, and he ate lunch downtown at Carney's. He was sitting at a corner table when a tall middle aged man suddenly appeared with a cup of coffee in his hands.

''I'm very sorry to impose, but would you mind sharing your table? Must be the rush hour around here.''

Frank motioned for the man to make himself at home. ''Salesman?'' he asked.

The man nodded, and quickly added, ''New territory. I'm just visiting a few businesses that look promising.''

''What's the product?''

''General business supplies,'' was the answer. ''I was just out to the baseball park. Thought they might be in the market for a few items.''

Frank stirred his coffee slowly. ''Talk with Greta Crim?''

''Say, I believe that was the lady's name. Real nice person. Mighty friendly. Can't say the same for the two gents out there. I guess they had a heap of important business to settle. Sure were down in the mouth.''

"You don't say."

"Yup, I do say. I'm no baseball fan. In fact, I never attended a game in my life, but I couldn't help but catch the drift of what was bothering those two. From what I gathered, they wanted to expand the ball club's operation — you know, move into a higher league. This George fellow, he was all for making the change, but he kept asking about some guy by the name of Knight. Said the change would never work without this guy on the payroll. Made the man behind the desk as mad as a hornet. He shouts, 'Knight's retired, and he won't change his mind. I told him we needed him, but he thinks he's a fisherman.' Well, they go back and forth for a few minutes, and then this George fellow gets up to leave. On the way out he says, 'Frank Knight's the best baseball scout in these parts. If we can't get him back, I'm for throwing out this entire deal.' The guy behind the desk slumped in his chair like a sick quail.''

Frank eyed the man carefully. He was about to pick up his check when the visitor added, "You know it's none of my business, but they sure could use some more tables in this place.''

At home Frank busied himself with a number of household chores. By four o'clock he chucked his varnish brush into a can of brush cleaner and grabbed his coat and hat. He walked to the ball park.

Harley was sitting behind his desk sorting through some papers. George Hauser lay on a narrow sofa, hat over his eyes, sound asleep. Frank slammed the door, and the manager popped up like a piece of toast.

"Geez! Frank, never wake up a man like that. I thought Harley had fallen off his chair or something.''

Frank grinned. "I've something to say, and I hope it meets with the approval of you two gents. I've been thinking about this "AA" move, and something tells me I should postpone my fishing for the time being. If you have a place for me on the payroll this summer, I'm ready to find those players we need. Got a blank contract in that drawer, Harley?"

"Frank, if I don't have, you can bet I'll find one before you change your mind."

"I hope my retirement lasts longer than that spell of yours, Frank." George seemed more than pleased with the sudden change of plans. "I hope all of us know what we're doing. Come September we may all be in retirement."

"Nonsense," shouted Harley. "We know what we have to do. The Atlantic League has a playoff system. If we can make fourth place, we make the post season playoffs. Gentlemen, that should be our goal — the first division. If Frank can find us some help in the pitching department and maybe a good hitter to boot, our boys are on their way. George here has some tricks to show those managers up north."

Frank asked, "George, how many of last year's pitchers are coming back?"

There was a moment's hesitation, and then the manager responded. "We have Doty, Zoltowski, Wyant, Welterroth, Codrington, and Travis signed. We released Crawford, Morton, and Ramsey. I've invited a couple of college pitchers to camp. They dropped out of school last fall. They have an outside chance to make the club, but with this step up, I would say their chances are mighty slim. Joel, of course, will be through high school in May. I've told him to keep in good shape and be ready to pitch when he reports. Any leads on talent you saw last year?"

"I saw a left-hander at Hanover who just might fill the bill. You know Hanover plays in the class "D" Southeastern League. Well, this kid was something like 4-10 with the Kings last season. They had a bad ball club, and this kid Gleason was always going up against the tough ball clubs. He was pretty discouraged by September. I know the manager over there, and he's no evaluater of pitchers. If Harley was to give them a call, he might be able to buy this kid."

7

Harley had already jotted the kid's name down and was reaching for the phone. In less than a minute he had the Hanover owner on the line.

"Mr. Pollard? Harley Walsh here. Say, we're looking for a left-hander to fill in a little this summer. We have a little money lying around this year; I thought you might have a southpaw we could take off your hands. We independent clubs have to help each other out, you know."

Harley listened intently for a few minutes, and then picked up the conversation. "Gleason, you say. Didn't have much of a record, did he?"

Harley winked at Frank and listened for the reply on the line. "Well, I'll tell you what I could do, Mr. Pollard. The kid apparently needs a great deal of work. I could take him off your hands for a cash payment of, let's say, $1,000.00. You had rather a rough season over there last year; maybe the money would be of some use to you this spring. How does that sound?"

There was a moments pause, and then Harley sang out, "Fine, fine, Mr. Pollard. Glad I could be of service. I'll give you another call on Monday, and we can arrange the paper work. Good day, Sir."

Harley was up and dancing around his desk. "Gentlemen, by the middle of next week we will have a new member of the club. Pete Gleason is about to be fitted to a Bear's uniform. I sure hope you're right about the kid's potential, Frank."

"Listen," cut in George, "if Frank likes the kid, I'm not going to lose any sleep over his potential. It's a big jump from "D" ball to "AA", but Frank would have never mentioned the kid unless he thought there was some hidden talent there. After Joel Travis I'm not about to question anything Frank suggests."

As Frank walked toward Henry Street, the late January wind blew the fine snow in all directions. The grass was hidden, the gate posts wore downy white caps, and the sidewalk before him was trackless. He stuffed his hands deep down into his pockets of his coat and wondered what Mary would say.

8

CHAPTER 2

SPRING TRAINING

Frank was standing just outside the batting cage, watching Burlington catcher Hal Meadowcroft take some warm up throws from right-hander Tom Wyant. He had just received some news from Harley that was about as easy to accept as a double shot of caster oil. The owner had decided to sell first baseman Henry Pearce to the "AAA" Coast League. It was a great opportunity for Henry, and Harley was not about to stand in the way of a player's progress. The big first baseman had been the power man for the Bears last season with 25 home runs and nearly 100 runs batted in. Frank knew the loss of Pearce could spell disaster for a club attempting to enter a higher class of minor league classification and competition. When Harley had informed George Hauser of the move, the manager threw up his hands and shouted, "Harley, you just sold half of our run output last year! How in the world can we make the first division with no power in the line up?"

Harley said nothing, but Frank had come to the owner's defense. "George, don't blame Harley. In fact, he handled the entire affair properly and aboveboard. Henry did a great job for us last year. You know, and I know, that we're here to help the players whenever we can. Pearce deserves the break."

George was quick to apologize. "I'm sorry, Harley. As usual, Frank's absolutely right."

Beyond that, they didn't talk about it very much; the disappointment went too deep for helpful discussion. Losing good ball players to higher classification clubs was just one of the hazzards of operating an independent ball club.

As left fielder Stuart Reems stepped into the batting cage, rain drops splattered down on the forepiece of Frank's cap, on the shoulders of his uniform, and on the papers attached to his clipboard. George Hauser shouted from the top step of the dugout: "Everybody hustle, now. We've got to get some work in today. Someone back up Wyant. Get a couple of towels out there to keep the balls dry."

Reems fouled several pitches off and then started to get some solid wood on the ball. Reems had been second to Pearce in home runs last season and had driven across 77 runs. The way the roster stood at present, Reems was a very important piece of property. The big outfielder had batted clean up last season and would probably remain in the fourth slot this season. Before he left the cage the veteran fly chaser drove a ball over the 390 mark in deep left center field.

As Frank was about to grab an infield fungo and give the infielders some work, he noticed a large shouldered man standing behind the batting cage. The man was dressed in an ugly gray suit which was much too small across the shoulders. The stranger wore a slightly soiled hat with the brim pushed down to the top of his ears. Frank felt he looked about as sloppy as the weather.

"Can I help you?" Frank asked.

There was a moment of heavy, threatening silence — then the man answered, "Maybe. You the manager of this outfit?"

"Afraid not," replied Frank. "That fellow over there in the dugout, George Hauser, he calls the shots."

The man grunted and stole a quick glance toward the dugout.

"Any objections to my watching a little batting practice?"

Frank was quick with his reply. "Any reason you can't sit in the stands?"

10

The man flashed a cold smile. When he spoke, his palid face showed arrogance. "Fans sit in stands. Ball players stand on the field. I'm no stub carrying fan; I'm a ball player. Look at all of those know it all's up there. Not a one of them knows anything about this game. Just because they spend a buck for a ticket they think they have the right to shout all their garbage."

Frank had too much to do to waste time with such a man. Before he went back to work, he informed the man he could stay behind the batting cage as long as he stayed out of the way of the players.

As the morning hours passed, Frank took turns at working with the infielders and outfielders. Shortly before noon, and lunch time, he found himself near the batting cage watching the last hitter take his swings. The stranger was still standing behind the cage.

As Frank studied Barney Kerr at the plate, the man walked toward him and asked flatly, "These the best hitters you got?"

Frank was getting fed up with the man's brashness. "Something wrong with 'em? Maybe you could do better?"

The man's lips twisted into a strange smile. "I haven't played on a ball club in three years, but I could put on a better show than any of those birds. Ping pong hitters, the most of them. The only guy you got with any power was that first one that hit. If you're going to start the season with all those little gnats, you better have four Walter Johnsons on your staff."

Frank set his jaw, and the back of his neck heated up. Before he thought about his words, they had escaped from his mouth, "Tell you what we better do. If we're in that much trouble, it would be a shame to let a fella like yourself get away without putting him in the cage. Might do wonders for all these weak hitters, you know, just watching what a real hitter looks like. How about coming over to the clubhouse after lunch, and I'll fix you up with a uniform?

Unless, of course, you're on a tight schedule?"

"I'm on no schedule," the man replied sharply, "and I'll be back with my shoes and bat within the hour."

In the clubhouse Frank felt like asking someone to give him a good swift kick. He had lost his composure completely. Here it was the first day of serious training, and he was wasting everybody's time with a bunch of nonsense. He found George Hauser in the training room.

When he explained the situation to the manager, George let out with a loud guffaw. "You mean this guy is actually going to stand in that cage and perform for us?"

"In the flesh," Frank replied.

"Well," said George, "let's hope he doesn't get conked on the noggin. After he's put on his show, we'll send him up to Harley!"

"Listen, George, this is no laughing matter. This guy is big enough and mean enough to wrestle a bear — and win! When he steps out of that cage, he'll probably be mad enough to whip half the club. I figure most of the guys will be rolling on the ground in hysterics. I'm going to give you the pleasure of telling him he's a no talent. I plan to make myself scarce."

Shortly before the lunch break ended, the brawny stranger walked into the clubhouse and started to undress in front of an empty locker. Frank got a spare uniform from the equipment room and handed it to the man. From a beat up old satchel he pulled a pair of scuffed up baseball spikes. Frank figured them to be about size 12's. In less than ten minutes the man pulled on the uniform, perched a wrinkled baseball cap on his head, and walked from the clubhouse.

Frank helped George organize the warmups, and then had Joe Codrington loosen up for some work on the mound. He thought he should mention who the first hitter would be. "Joe, we have a fellow working out today. He's going to take a little hitting practice

12

this afternoon. Just throw good batting practice speed and throw strikes. I'm sure he won't be in there long.''

Codrington nodded and walked to the mound to finish his warmup. Frank went to locate his antagonist.

The man was doing some exercises behind the batting cage.

''I suppose you're a bit rusty, not having played on a ball club of late. Should I ask our pitcher to soft toss a few until you get your timing straightened away?''

The man glared and answered gruffly, ''Have him throw his best stuff if he wants. Makes no difference to me.'' Picking up a long black bat, he made for the cage. Before stepping in, he yelled out to Codrington, ''Throw that junk in here and then protect yourself!'' The Bears' right-hander paid no attention to the remark and concentrated on delivering a strike to the plate.

The first pitch sailed outside, and the right hand hitter took the offering. The next pitch was in the strike zone, but the man did not swing. Codrington yelled, ''How do you want it? Served up on a platter?''

''Just keep throwing rookie,'' the man shot back. ''You'll know by the sound of the bat when it's in here.''

Frank was feeling more uneasy by the minute. If Harley ever walked from his office and saw what was going on — there just might be a manager and a scout looking for another job.

Codrington put a little extra on the next pitch. The ball came in around belt high, and the stranger brought the black bat around with authority. There was a sharp crack, and the ball jumped off the wood. There was never the slightest doubt that the drive would clear the left center field fence. After watching the ball disappear, the players in the field looked to the plate to take a closer look at the hitter. Codrington pulled another ball from his hip pocket and fired it to the plate. The man stepped into the pitch and lined it viciously down the left field line. The following offering was hit far and deep to straight away center field. Carl Zoltowski went back to the 410 mark and watched it sail over the barrier.

Frank studied the strong man with the massive shoulders. He had good moves at the plate. He kept his head still, and his swing was short and powerful. His hands were away from his body, and Frank was willing to bet that they were quick. This fellow was no stranger to a batters' box. With that swing he could hit the ball out of any ball park in the country.

"I'd say our stranger has a little power." George had come around behind the cage.

"So it seems," Frank answered. "This guy is probably pushing 40 years of age. I would wager he's put a great many of those baseballs over the fence within the past 20 years or so. Wonder where he's from, or where he's played his baseball."

George shrugged. "Get him out of the cage and we'll ask him a few questions."

Frank yelled, "Next hitter!" and the man walked slowly from the hitting structure. George called him over and introduced himself.

"I guess you've met Frank Knight here. Frank does the scouting for the club. I didn't catch the name, or where you're from."

"Name's Luther Barber. I'm staying over on the coast."

George studied the long black bat. "Quite a war club you got there. Must be 36 inches, carrying 40 or more ounces."

The man nodded, but offered nothing else.

Frank entered the conversation with, "How much professional baseball have you played?"

The man snapped, "That's my business. I signed my last baseball contract three years ago, and I got my release in writing at the close of the season. I got me a job up north on the docks, and I haven't been near a ball park since the close of the war. I heard your ball club was training here in Auburn; one of my buddies up in Monticello mentioned it to me. I've no love for baseball, but I just got laid off, and the prospects of getting back to work this summer are mighty slim. I can carry this ball club with my bat, but I'm not begging for no job. If you want me to work out with the club until the pitchers' arms are in shape, I'll be here. I know what you're thinking. You're thinking this guy is a great batting practice hitter, but just wait till the pitchers start throwing the breaking stuff. Well, I hit curveballs better than the fast stuff. When your staff feels ready, they can throw me their best. Makes no difference to me."

"Mind telling us your age?" George asked the question bluntly.

"I'll be forty in August. Makes no difference. I could hit the guys in this league out of a wheel chair!"

The rain was coming a little heavier now, and George was about to call it a day. "Tell you what, Luther. You report here tomorrow morning. Let's say a bit before nine o'clock. Bring a suitcase with you, and we'll fix you up at the hotel. Work out with the club, and we'll see what develops. How does that sound?"

Luther nodded his head slowly, then added, "I don't want any favors from anybody, and I don't want people around here poking their noses into my business. If I decide to join this outfit, you'll get your money's worth and then some. One more thing — I room alone. I don't want some foolish rookie bending my ear." He then turned on his heel and headed for the clubhouse.

When the man had left, George said, "That guy's mad at the whole world. I've got the feeling, though, that he's not as mean and cantankerous as he wants everybody to believe. Right now I'm only sure of one thing. The man can drive a baseball with some kind of power — power that we need on this club."

"Right," Frank agreed, "but we don't even know what position he plays. He had me so worked up this morning that I forgot to ask him."

"For the present, Frank, it doesn't matter. If he can hit the way he says he can, we could carry him for pinch-hitting. With his size, I would say the man is probably a first baseman or maybe a left fielder. His fingers are in too good a shape to be a catcher."

Frank nodded in agreement. "You know, of course, what our big problem will be. With this guy's disposition he'll probably have all the players steamed up before they leave the clubhouse."

"If that's the case, I mean if the man's a troublemaker, he'll be repacking that suitcase in a hurry."

The rain had slackened, and Frank went back to his work with the infielders. George had picked up an outfield fungo bat and was shouting to some of the pitchers. "Time for running — loosen those legs up — everybody take his turn — come on, Welterroth, you're my first victim." George hit a long flyball in right center, and the Bear right-hander was off and running.

CHAPTER

3

FIRST SACKER

Three days after the arrival of Luther Barber, George Hauser noticed a very slim, deferential, timid looking gentleman with a white mustache sitting in the stands behind the first base dugout. The man was dressed in splendor, and showed up in the crowd like a flamingo in a chicken run. Just before the break for lunch, George was surprised to see the visitor talking with none other than Luther Barber. The two were huddled in conversation at the gate which led to the runway behind home plate. As George yelled, "Pick everything up; we're through for this morning. Everybody back out here in one hour," Luther and the man shook hands, and the big first baseman walked slowly toward the clubhouse.

George and Frank had decided that Luther should be offered a contract. For the past few days the big strongman had been powdering the ball to all parts of the outfield. He had a slightly uppercut swing, and it seemed everything he hit was either a line drive or a towering flyball which carried, in most cases, well over the fence. His work at first base had been adequate. He caught the ball well, and his arm was strong enough to make the double play. The longest throw a first baseman has to make is the one to third base, and Luther could fire the ball for this rather short distance. He was no gazelle around the bag, and now and then he would get his feet tangled up, but, all in all, his work had been acceptable. In the clubhouse and on the field he was about as friendly as a spooked rattlesnake, but neither George or Frank could say he had caused any trouble. He had worked hard and kept to himself.

As George was enjoying a ham and cheese sandwich, Harley came storming into the manager's compartment. He quickly closed the door behind him and grabbed a chair which he pulled up before the manager. "George, we've got problems!" came the harsh voice. "What's your evaluation of Luther Barber?"

"As a player?"

"Yes, of course."

"Well, Frank and I talked it over last evening. We both decided you should put him under contract. We, of course, haven't seen him against any conditioned pitching arms, but Frank believes the guy might prove to be the best power hitter in the league. He hit some balls out here yesterday that

17

were unreal. With Pearce gone, this guy could really fill the bill at first base."

Harley twisted in his chair and drew a weary breath; when he spoke, the words were slow and deliberate. "I think we've lost him. This morning I noticed Vance Neuberger up in the stands. I think he was out here yesterday, too, but I'm not sure. Neuberger's working for a club in the Pacific Coast League. It's been several years since I've seen the man, but I'd know him any place. He always dresses like a German Count. I read in one of the sporting publications that he was working out on the coast. He has to be in this area looking for talent."

"You think he's looking at Luther?" George asked.

"I know he's looking at Luther. The two of them were talking this morning. I say let's get Barber in here right now and talk turkey with him. Maybe, just maybe, we can beat Neuberger to the punch."

"I'm puzzled about Barber," George confessed. "Where in the world has this guy been playing baseball? He lays off for two or three seasons and still hits the ball like he's in mid season form. He walks in here a nobody, and now a guy from AAA baseball apparently has him under wraps. The guy is pushing 40, yet Neuberger must think he can still play in a league which is just a shade below the big time. Have you seen his written release?"

"Obviously I haven't. I'll have to see it of course before I sign him."

"If you sign him," George replied.

Harley nodded, and went to get the big first baseman. Before George could finish his sandwich, Harley and Luther were coming through the doorway.

"Grab a chair, Luther," Harley's voice was quite calm. "Won't keep you long. Just a little business that needs attending to."

Luther frowned, but said nothing.

Harley started with, "Luther, I've just had a talk with George concerning your future with the club.

He, along with Frank, feel that you're the man to take over the chores at first base. George needs some power in the line up, and he's willing to gamble that you can hit the hard stuff once the season starts. I've typed up a contract, and I'd like to have you take a look at it.'' The owner paused a moment to remove the document from his inside coat pocket. He then passed it over to the player for his inspection.

Barber took less than 20 seconds to scan the contract. He then handed it back to Harley without comment.

"Well?"

"I don't like it!"

"What don't you like?" asked the owner.

"I don't like those figures that say how big my pay checks are supposed to be each month."

Harley pulled his weight up out of the chair. The player's reply came as no big surprise. With Neuberger hanging around, Harley figured Barber would try to hold him up for more money — a great deal more money. Walking toward the door, the owner shot back a parting comment. "Luther, I'd like to have you on this ball club, but just because Vance Neuberger happens to be camped out in our ball park doesn't give you a license to hold me up. This contract calls for $300.00 per month, and that's a fair offer. Neuberger can talk double that if he wants to, but you'll never get that kind of money from me. I don't bid for ball players." Harley jerked the door shut.

George had been watching Luther Barber for the past several minutes. As Harley stormed from the room, the big man neither changed his expression or moved a muscle in his massive frame.

"Neuberger?" asked George. "Would you say he's a bit unethical for hanging around another man's ball park with the sole purpose of stealing unsigned players?" George thought it was worth a try to draw Luther out of his shell.

"None of my business," he answered, "if the guy bends the rules. It's been my experience that owners can take care of themselves."

George pushed the subject a little farther. "What's your impression of Harley, Luther? Would you say he's a straight shooter? A man of his word?"

Luther stared at the veteran skipper. "Can't say. All I know is what I hear; don't place much importance on hearsay."

"Neuberger offer you a contract?"

"What if he did!"

"More than Harley offered?"

Luther snorted, "A lot more. If you doubt my word go up and ask him."

George shook his head. "I've no reason to doubt your word, Luther. I suppose you'll be pulling up stakes and moving along with Neuberger?"

For a time Luther sat thumping the fingers of his right hand on the armrest of his chair. When he spoke, he seemed a bit more friendly. "I'm not leaving with Neuberger or anyone else. People around here have treated me all right; I'm not complaining. In fact, I rather like the place. Neuberger offered me $500.00 a month." Reaching into his back pocket he withdrew a rumpled piece of paper and tossed it on the manager's desk. "You tell Walsh to make out a contract for $400.00 a month, and I'll sign it. If anyone's getting held up in this deal, it's me. He had no right to talk to me like that!"

George looked at the figures on the paper. After a moment's silence, he resumed the conversation. "Don't be too hard on Harley. The longer you stay around the more respect you'll have for the man. Trying to make ends meet on an independent club can cause any man to lose his temper now and then. I'll talk with him this afternoon regarding the contract. If I know Harley, he'll give you that $400.00 per month, and he'll appreciate your loyalty to the ball club. It's very important to everyone around here to make a decent showing in the Atlantic League. It's going to be a rough haul to make the play-offs. Maybe you're the fellow we need to grab fourth place.''

The big man managed a thin smile. ''Why settle for fourth place? I'm no braggart; I back up what I say. Put me in the clean-up position and I'll drive in between 125 and 150 runs for the club. All I ask is that those slap hitters get on base in front of me. Put a good hitter behind me, like that Reems guy; that way they can't pitch around me. I figure the first month of the season will be a picnic. None of those pitchers up there will know how to pitch me. They're going to feed me fastballs for awhile, then go to the breaking stuff. I'm a better fastball hitter, but by the second month it won't matter what they serve up. By May the ball starts looking like a watermelon to me. I'm not asking for favors, just a chance to drive in the runs.''

George grinned, ''Don't worry about the opportunity to drive across base runners. If you prove you can hit with men on, you're going to be swinging from the time you leave the dugout. I'll consider what you said about Stuart Reems. My guess would be I'll have either Reems or Miller behind you in the line up. Again, all of this conversation is based on the hope that you'll be able to do the job. I can't imagine your stepping into a league such as the Atlantic League and having a season like you just described. I can't imagine it, but I'm not saying it couldn't happen. Confidence in oneself is a great equalizer for adversity.''

Luther's voice dropped and mellowed slightly, ''I'm not much on big words like you just used, but I know what you're saying. I've yet to see the pitcher who had the stuff to overmatch me at the plate. I respect good pitchers, but eventually I catch up with all of those guys. Plenty of players, teammates, never liked me because I've always had all that confidence, and I made no bones about it. I don't see the harm in saying you're good if you can back it up on the field. I haven't made a single friend on this club, maybe won't all season, but by midseason all of them will know I mean what I say. Makes no difference to me if they like me or not. I'm asking for no favors."

George lifted himself from his chair, then walked over and slapped the big first baseman on the back. "You get back out on the field and get some work around the bag. Maybe we can get your contract all straightened out by the time you leave the park this afternoon. Remember, if you have a beef about something, come in and discuss the problem with me before airing the complaint in the dugout."

Shortly before three o'clock George divided the players up and held a three inning practice game. On one club he had Miller at third, Kerr at short, Wilkins at second, Barber at first, and Meadowcroft behind the plate. In the outfield he stationed Reems in left, Goodman in center, and McCoy in right. Three pitchers, Wyant, Doty, and Welterroth, were to work one inning each. On the other club, Pete Gleason, Codrington, and Zoltowski were set for brief mound duty, and Wickland was behind the plate.

In the top of the first inning the club, managed by Frank Knight, pushed across two runs. Wilkins leading off, doubled, and Kerr singled him home. Goodman struck out, but Barber kept the inning going with a walk. Stuart Reems tripled into right center bringing Barber home with the second run. Miller popped out, and McCoy closed the inning out with a flyball to left.

Tom Wyant was not throwing hard. He was concentrating on throwing strikes and working himself into shape. The second stringers loaded the bases in the bottom of the first on three singles. Ken Lambert, George's best utility ballplayer, then lined a double in the gap sending across three runs. At the close of one complete inning the score stood at 4-2 with Hauser's club on top.

Codrington put the regulars down in order in the top of the second. In the bottom half of the inning Doty struck out Wickland with two runners on base, and the game moved into the final inning.

With right-hander Zoltowski on the hill, Wilkins grounded out second to first. Kerr popped out, but

Jack Goodman laced a single up the middle. Luther Barber stepped into the right hand batter's box.

Zoltowski, a slim right hander, looked down to Wickland for his sign. The first delivery was a curveball to the outside of the plate, and Barber took a vicious swing at the pitch, fouling the ball back over the stands. Zoltowski took his time before looking down to Wickland for his next sign. As he swung into his stretch position, Barber dug in at the plate. The pitch was a letter high fastball that ran toward the hitter. Barber was sent sprawling in the dirt. In an instant he was on his feet and, with his bat, started for the mound. George Hauser jumped off the bench and ran toward the middle of the infield. Frank Knight was already out of the other dugout. By the time they reached the pitching area, Barber had said something to Zoltowski and was headed back to the batters box.

George approached the pitcher. "What's going on, Zolty?"

"Not much." replied the reliefer. "For a minute there I felt like calling for help, but that big moose just walked out here and paid me a compliment."

"He didn't threaten your life?"

The veteran pitcher smiled. "Not in the least. He just pointed that big black bat at me and says, 'Takes guts to knock me down. That was the best purpose pitch I've seen down here all spring. I'll tell you something though, Slim. You better have something on the next strike you throw.' George, that Barber guy is some kind of odd character!"

When the inning had ended, and the players in the field had seated themselves in the dugout, the fun started. Wickland piped up with, "Did you hear little Joe Meyers out at second base? He was yelling 'Hold me back! Hold me back!' Funny thing, though, his feet weren't moving!"

Ken Lambert had something to say to Wickland. "I've always said you're a smart catcher, Wicky. Today you were very smart. All during that episode you were intelligent enough to keep your mask on!"

"Listen," replied Wickland, "we can joke all we want, but for a few seconds there I was worried. I was thinking about tackling that blacksmith before he tore poor Zolty apart. I was about to make my move when he started talking instead of swinging."

Lambert winked at Hauser. "Tell me Wicky, did you mention to Luther that you called for a knock-down pitch?"

The catcher paused for a moment before replying. "Wouldn't you know it, Kenny? I plumb forgot!" Then, getting serious, he added, "Listen, Lambert, there's no way I'm going to call for that kind of pitch in a game between ourselves. Zoltowski made the decision on his own, and I'm not saying it was good judgment. Barber showed me plenty out there. I'm not sure I would have reacted in the same manner. That pitch nearly peeled the buttons off Barber's shirt."

Welterroth set George's team down in order in the bottom of the third. All the players did a full lap around the field and headed for the clubhouse, Frank Knight and the manager were the last ones to leave the field.

"You know," offered George, "Barber has some of these players confused. They still don't trust him; they don't even like him, but they're taking another look at him. It's a beginning."

Frank nodded. His voice seemed unsteady. "It could have been a nasty situation this afternoon. Barber went more than half way to keep the peace. One of these days the players will have to travel the same route. If they don't, we're headed for trouble."

CHAPTER

4

GRAPEFRUIT SEASON

Luther lay very still in the darkness, his heart thumping severely, fighting to escape from the reality of his nightmare. It seemed he always woke up at exactly the same place in this haunting dream. His loving wife Cathy had just passed away from that lingering illness, an illness she had fought gallantly until there was not a single strain of reserve strength left.

For months after his great loss, he had walked the streets not knowing or caring where his feet might carry him. Eventually the long winter darkness had rolled away, but the bitterness remained. When he lost his wife, he was between baseball contracts; the 1938 season seemed very unimportant. As it turned out, it was well past spring training before he decided to answer a call from the Austin, Texas, ball club. When the season started, he took his frustration out on the opposing pitchers. He pounded the ball against and over every fence in the Texas League. He became a loner on and off the field. He insisted on rooming alone, and each road hotel room was a God forsaken outpost. He would lie upon his room bed for several hours. Then he would shut his eyes tight. He could feel a moving, roaring wave of feeling that pounded his body until he felt beaten and injured. No one could imagine how very much he missed his wife. It was odd, the things he remembered. His life had crumbled suddenly and left him standing there, alone. He remembered the important things, the big things, but he also remembered the little things: the way his wife's hand touched him, many times he was too busy to notice; her voice, always soft and caring; the way she carefully and quietly carried out her household duties when he needed an hour or so of peaceful sleep.

Now, ten years later, he found sleep an elusive item. He had been sitting upright in his bed for nearly two hours, and now slow gray dawn began to crawl into the room. He pulled himself up and draggedly made his rounds. When he left the hotel room, his watch read twenty minutes past the seventh hour.

Downstairs he crossed the hotel foyer and bought a morning paper from the room clerk. By the time he had read through the sports pages, it was time for breakfast. As he was walking into the small dining room, he heard a voice call his name.

"Luther, wait up!" Shortstop Barney Kerr came striding across the hotel lobby. "Mind a partner for breakfast?"

"Suit yourself." Luther answered.

Kerr led the way to a table near the center of the room. After ordering, Luther went back to his paper.

"Luther, all the players were pleased to hear that you've signed a contract with Mr. Walsh. When all of us heard about this "AA" stuff we were sort of skeptic. Quite a jump up for an entire bunch of ballplayers. Burlington has the best fans in the league, and we sure wanted to put a competitive club on the field. When I came down here, I don't mind saying I was worried. The club then lost Henry Pearce, the best power man on the roster." Kerr paused for a moment, then continued, "When you showed up and started hitting those long drives over the fence, everybody started perking up. I just want to say you've lifted spirits up around here, Luther; lifted everybody's hopes to the point where we're starting to believe that maybe, just maybe, we can make those playoffs in September."

Laying his paper down, Luther studied the little infielder. He liked the bespectacled Burlington shortstop. He had never seen an infielder who wore eye glasses, but it certainly had no ill effects on Kerr's performance in the field and at the plate. Together with Wilkins, they made up one of the smoothest double-play combinations he had ever witnessed.

"Save your compliments until after the season starts." The big first baseman's voice was low and friendly. "Spring training never means very much. Just a time and place to get into good playing shape. When the bell rings up north, it's a new ball game. I plan to hit at least a dozen home runs the first month. If you want the club to get off to a good start, I would suggest that you and Wilkins make sure you're on base when I hit those homers. Three run homers look a lot better in the box score than those solo shots."

Barney Kerr was warming up to the big man. "Luther, I believe what you're saying. You're not just fanning the breeze; you really believe you're going to unload those home runs. One litte thing bothers me, though. How can you be so sure those opposing pitchers are going to co-operate?"

Luther smiled, "Doesn't matter if they co-operate or not. Once they let go of the ball, and I hit it over the fence, it's in the box score. You can't erase an official box score."

Kerr leaned forward, entirely wrapped up in the conversation. "Where did you learn to hit with so much confidence?"

"Confidence comes with performance. I found out years ago that no pitcher could throw a fastball by me. Many pitchers are dumb and stubborn. You hit their best fastball over the fence and they come right back with another one. They can't believe that anyone can handle their best pitch like that." Luther continued, "For awhile I had trouble with breaking pitches, but I saw so many of them that I eventually got to the point where I could hit a good curveball as well as a fastball. I'm not saying I never get fooled; I am saying it doesn't happen too often."

After finishing their meal, the two players signed

their checks and walked from the dining room. Before parting, Barney Kerr turned to the big man and said, "Luther, I've enjoyed our talk. Don't lose all that self confidence. I hope a little of that stuff can rub off on me." He was off with a bound, whistling a pretty tune that Luther had heard some place before.

2

George Hauser posted the starting line up for the afternoon exhibition game.

Wilkins, 2b

Kerr, ss

McCoy, rf

Barber, 1b

Reems, lf

Miller, 3b

Goodman, cf

Meadowcroft, c

Wyant, p

The opposition was Madison Heights, a club in the Northeast League. As the Burlington team took the field, a sweltering heat settled down over the little field.

Wyant got the first hitter on a routine flyball to Goodman in center field. After giving up a single, he got the third hitter to hit a sharp grounder directly at Eddie Wilkins. Feeding Kerr a nice throw, the double play was turned over in plenty of time. In the home half the Bears went down in one, two, three order. In the top of the second Jack Goodman was forced to make a diving catch in right center, preventing two runs from scoring. Goodman made a habit of robbing opposing hitters with such catches. Always getting a good jump on the ball, he reached drives that looked like sure hits when they left the bat.

Luther led off the home second and worked the count to three balls and two strikes. The husky right-hander sent a good live fastball at the strike zone. Barber caught the pitch solidly and hit a tremendous drive over the 400 foot marker in nearly straight away center field. George Hauser could not remember when he had seen a pitch hit any harder. The drive was not a flyball, but a line shot that just kept carrying until it disappeared over the fence. As Barber circled the bases, several of the Burlington players on the bench sat discussing the force of the blow. When the first baseman reached the plate, a number of players were there to greet him. On the bench Barney Kerr slid in beside the first sacker. "Geeze, what a way to flatten a baseball! Was it a fastball, Luther?"

"A real cripple," answered Luther. "My Aunt Sarah could have hit that pitch out. He should have thrown a breaking ball or maybe a change pitch. He might have known I was looking for a fat fastball. A real dumb pitch."

Kerr laughed loudly, "Well, look at it this way, Luther. You gave him a nice education on just one delivery. He's bound to be a better pitcher after that lesson. Should make you feel good, deep down inside."

Luther smiled, "We'll see how much education he got when I hit next time. Wouldn't surprise me if he tried to sneak another fastball by me."

Kerr shook his head. "After that clothesline, you'll be lucky if you see another fastball all afternoon."

The game moved right along through the middle innings. By the top of the seventh a little breeze had moved in to make playing conditions a little more tolerable. The Bears hung on to a 3-1 lead.

Wyant and Codrington had held the opposition to just five hits. Pete Gleason took over the mound duties in the seventh. He got a bad break when a ground ball took a high hop over Chet Miller's glove. The left-hander struck out the next hitter, but a little right-hand batter punched a double down the right field line. With men on second and third, Gleason missed on a three and two pitch to load the bases. The next hitter sent a hard ground ball toward right field. Luther threw himself at the ball and made a nice stop of the grass burner. Throwing to Gleason, the hitter was retired. With the score standing at 3-2, the little lefty worked hard to retire the next hitter, but it was not to be. The slim right-hand batter drove a line drive up the left center field alley, and both base runners scored easily. The Madison Heights club had taken a 4-3 lead.

A side-arming right-hander had taken over the mound chores for the visitors. He whipped the ball in like the pitch was coming from the shortstop's position. The Burlington right-hand hitters were giving in to his pitches. When they did make contact, it was the result of a weak swing. The side-armer threw hard, and more than once he had came inside to send a Burlington hitter into the dirt. No one was

digging in on this sidewinder.

Zoltowski came on in the ninth and managed to keep the score close. The Bears were down 5-3 going into the last of the ninth.

Eddie Wilkins led off and dropped a better than average bunt down the third base line, but the Madison Heights third baseman rose to the occasion and threw him out. Barney Kerr kept fouling pitches off until he drew a base on balls. McCoy got caught leaning back from a good fastball and was called out on strikes. Luther Barber walked slowly toward the plate. Kerr yelled in encouragement from first base.

Luther dug his feet in firmly as the right-hander took his sign. The first pitch was a riding side-armed fastball that sent the first baseman down in the dirt. Several Burlington players shouted angrily from the top step of the dugout. When Luther regained his feet, his perspiration soaked uniform was caked with the red dirt around the batter's box.

After taking a lengthy stretch position the tall right-hander uncorked another fastball that again sent Luther sprawling in the dust. George Hauser took several steps toward the plate umpire and yelled, "Make him throw the ball around the plate! That's your responsibility, ump! Get out there before someone gets hurt!"

The umpire took off his mask and started toward the dugout. Halfway he shouted at the manager, "Listen, Hauser, get back in the dugout! If I want your advice, I'll ask for it!"

George returned to the dugout steps, but he let go with another blast at the arbitrator. "If you think I'm going to stand here and see my players thrown at, you're crazy. Get control of the game!" The umpire pulled on his mask and yelled, "Let's play ball!"

Luther again dug his feet into the batter's box. Taking his time the Madison Heights pitcher took a long stretch and brought his delivery toward the plate. The pitch was a side-armed curveball. The right-hander started the offering behind the big

31

slugger. As the ball broke over the plate, Luther kept his normal hitting stance in the batter's box. At first base, Kerr watched as Luther brought the bat around with a powerful swing. There was a resounding crack as the fat part of the bat met the ball. Every player on and off the field knew the ball was gone when it left the big black piece of wood. Kerr was jumping and running at the same time. He was still yelling and waving his cap as he approached third base. Every single Bear player was moving toward the plate. Luther, in his slow natural gait, was making his way around the bases. His head was down, and he never once looked at the Madison Heights pitcher. As he headed down toward home plate, George Hauser grabbed his hand and gave the big man a slap on the number of his uniform. Several of the Bear players went up the line to offer their congratulations. Most had never seen a man dropped twice at the plate, only to get up and hit a home run over the fence. Ball players don't forget those kinds of performances.

The Bears won the contest in the 10th. inning on doubles by Chet Miller and Hal Meadowcroft. A smallish left-hander had taken over for the side-armer, and Burlington scored in a hurry. After Barber's exhibition there was no way the game was going to get away from the Bear players.

In the clubhouse Luther undressed slowly, letting the other players do the talking. When Tom Wyant asked him about the pitch he had hit for the second home run, he merely shrugged his massive shoulders. He took his shower without a comment to anyone.

Barney Kerr was sitting in front of his locker as the first baseman left the shower-room. Luther paused for a minute to sit down next to the skinny infielder. ''As I told you this morning, there's no use hitting home runs in most cases unless someone's perched on the bases. Rather clever the way you kept fouling off those pitches till you got a walk. I never paid much attention to that type of hitting before. Don't show as much in the box score, but it's just about as important as driving the ball over the

fence.'' With a slight smile, the man with the big body pulled himself up from the bench and returned to his locker.

Barney Kerr was nearly dressed when he noticed Luther walking slowly toward the door of the dimly lighted clubhouse. He was hardly picking up his feet, kind of shuffling along, and his hat was pulled down close around his head. Barney knew a troubled man when he saw one. It wasn't the lines in a person's forehead that indicated worry. It was the little things, thrown in with the larger things, that gave a person away. Luther Barber had lost the slightest spring in his step. He felt sorry for the big slugger. He wished he knew more about the man's past.

CHAPTER
5

A WHALE OR A MINNOW

Greta Crim could play a fast little tune on her typewriter. She had been in the employment of the Burlington Ball Club for nearly ten seasons. Greta was smarter than two whips. She possessed a sparkling personality, and when she talked you listened, and you had a swell time doing it. She had been raised in the eastern part of the country, and educated at a pleasant little girls' school in New Hampshire. Teaching had not appealed to her, so after receiving her degree she came back home and sent up a trial balloon. She informed her parents that she was going to give the world of baseball a whirl. She had been an avid baseball fan ever since her grandfather, an old time catcher, had shown her his minor league clippings. After viewing those articles, she had read everything she could lay her hands on about professional baseball. She discovered that minor league baseball was founded by James A. Williams of Columbus, Ohio. The date was February 20, 1877, and the league James founded was the International Association.

Greta happened to spot an advertisement in the Sporting News one afternoon. The ad stated that a Mr. Harley Walsh was looking for someone to handle general office work. Mr. Walsh was sole owner of a minor league club called the Burlington Bears. She sent a letter stating her qualifications, and one week later she had the position.

Recently Greta had been following the adventures of one Luther Barber. Like others connected with the operation of the club, she had been worried when

Henry Pearce packed his bags and left for California. She considered herself a good judge of baseball talent. Until Barber arrived, she would have bet her year's wages that Burlington was destined for second division status. Now she was not so sure. The crack of Luther's bat could nearly be heard through the thick walls of the front office building. She knew all about those gigantic home runs, but like everyone else she knew little about the man himself. He had visited the office but twice and had only nodded his head in greeting to her.

Greta was sorting through some papers when a middle-aged man entered the office. He wore gray slacks and a checkered coat. His tie was loosened.

"May I help you?"

"I believe you can," the man answered. "I came in this morning from Gulfport. My editor caught wind of some odd happenings down here the other day. This guy Barber had quite an afternoon at the plate." The man chuckled, and continued, "When the boss mentioned this assignment, I could have cared less. Baseball bores me, but, when he brought up Barber's name, I got interested in a hurry. Funny thing, I never thought our paths would cross again."

Greta studied the stranger. "You know Luther Barber?"

"Like the back of my hand," the man said calmly.

Greta looked away. Then she said in a quiet voice, "The ball club's on the road today. Maybe I could give you information you need for your story."

The man shook his head. "I'm in no hurry. It's Barber that I'm interested in interviewing. The last time I saw him was right after he lost his wife. Couple of us went up to Tulsa to offer our condolences. Barber threw both of us out the front door. I never saw him after that, but I heard he went to the Texas League. One of my friends out west wrote a couple of articles about him in later years. He apparently became a real loner. A sportswriter's nightmare. He jumped around from club to club, always having trouble with managers and players.

From the time he lost his wife, the guy made a complete nuisance of himself."

A swathe of bright sunlight entered the windows of the little office room. Greta moved to a nearby desk, where she opened a small notebook. "If you want to give me your name and where you're staying, I'll make sure Mr. Barber receives the information. The ball club should be arriving back here by early evening."

"Name's Paul Morran. I'm staying just outside of town; place called Kelly's. What's the club schedule for tomorrow?"

Greta answered the question without looking up. "We're home for an afternoon game with Cambridge. Two o'clock starting time."

When Greta lifted her head, the man was gone. She had not cared for the newspaper man's appearance and attitude. She was sure he had an ax to grind.

Picking up the phone, she placed a call to the ball park at St. Charles. She left word with the office that Harley Walsh was to return her call as soon as possible. An hour later the Bears' owner was on the line.

"Greta, what in the world's so darn important that I have to be bothered in the middle of a ball game?"

"Don't be stuffy," she answered. "Something has come up, and I'm not sure how we should handle the situation. I may be over reacting, but I felt you should know about the newspaper man who walked in here a few minutes ago. He knows Luther Barber!"

There was a moment's silence on the line. "Knows him from where?"

"He met Barber years ago in Oklahoma. Tulsa, I believe he said. Luther had just lost his wife. This guy, his name is Paul Morran, had a run-in with Barber over an interview. Our first baseman threw him out in the street."

"And you feel this Morran fellow wants to stir up trouble?"

36

Without hesitation Greta gave her reply. "I'm sure of it. He admitted that baseball bored him. You don't take the time and the expense to make the trip over here from Gulfport just to yawn away the day. If I were you, I'd mention this character to Luther. Our Mr. Morran plans to be out here tomorrow afternoon."

"Greta, I'm glad you called. This could be a whale or a minnow, but at least we have a little time to decide what our next move will be. I'll talk with Luther after the game; he might have a suggestion about how to handle this guy. Why in blue blazes do these things always happen when things are starting to fall into place! Luther's just starting to wear these opposing pitchers out. He drove another ball out of the park in the first inning this afternoon." There was a heavy sigh on the owner's end of the line.

Greta felt sorry for her boss. She realized how very much he wanted to field a competitive club back in Burlington. Losing Luther Barber, the way he was hitting, would demoralize the entire ball club. She lifted and lightened the tone of her voice. "Cheer up, boss; things will work out. You had best get back to the field. See you here in the morning."

Harley sat in the office like a wooden man, staring straight ahead, completely motionless. The last person he wanted to see was some snooping, egotistical sportswriter. He had experienced a number of bad encounters with such people. Most writers on the sports beat were fair and admirable people. Now and then, however, you ran across a member who must have been asleep when the editor passed out the official code of journalistic ethics. Sensationalism meant more to this individual than reporting the facts.

By the time he returned to the ball game, the Bears were hitting in the top of the eighth inning. The score stood at 5-4, and Burlington was on the short side of the total run production. He had hardly lowered himself into his seat when Chet Miller grounded into a quick double play, ending the top of the frame.

Jim Doty walked to the mound to work the bottom of the eighth. The big right-hander looked sharp as he retired three batters in order. Harley could hear Frank Knight yelling encouragement to the Burlington players as they came off the field. Meadowcroft could be seen at the edge of the dugout. He tossed his catching equipment aside and grabbed a bat. A minute or two later he was in the batter's box facing a tall southpaw.

Meadowcroft hit the ball hard, but it was a line drive that hung up just long enough for the center fielder to make the catch. Ken Lambert walked to the plate, pinch-hitting for Doty. Lambert took a strike, and then flied out to right field. Harley thought about making his way to the clubhouse.

Wilkins worked the count to 3-2 before singling up the middle. Barney Kerr took a couple of hard practice swings before stepping in to hit. On the first pitch he dumped a perfect bunt down the third base line. Kerr got a good jump out of the box and beat the third baseman's throw by half a step. Harley had a great deal of admiration for Barney Kerr. If there was a way to get on base, old Barney would find it. There was no such thing as being too aggressive in baseball. You couldn't be any more aggressive than the Burlington shortstop.

McCoy, the Bear's right fielder dug in at the plate. After getting ahead in the count, the southpaw fooled around and got cute with his pitches. McCoy ran the string to three balls and two strikes. The next fastball sailed high, and McCoy trotted down to first. Luther Barber, swinging three bats, tossed two white ones aside and walked slowly to the plate with his black piece of lumber. Harley felt a chill break through him. There was something about Barber that spelled excitement on the ball field.

Noticing a man with a scorecard sitting in the next row, Harley asked the fan, "Could you tell me what this hitter has done this afternoon?" The fan ran a finger across the scorecard. "Homered in the first; grounded out in the third; doubled in the fifth;

doubled again in the seventh." The well dressed man smiled, "The way this guy hits I wouldn't be a bit surprised if they walked him, sending across the tying run, and then took their chances with the next hitter. Can't say I ever saw that type of strategy, but this guy looks like some kind of hitter."

The home-club manager had seen enough of his big southpaw and waved a right-hander in from the bullpen. Luther stood off to the side of the plate and awaited the new pitcher. When the reliefer started his warmup pitches, the burly first baseman studied his every move, when he stepped into the box to hit, Harley's chills returned.

The right-hander looked the runner back to third, and then went into a quick compact wind-up. The pitch popped across the outside corner for a called strike. Luther looked as though he was taking the pitch all the way. Upon return of the ball, the pitcher heaved a big sigh and looked down for the second sign. Luther never moved his feet in the box. His head was still, and his eyes studied the hurler.

The next pitch was a straight change, and it was a beauty. Luther took a hard swing, but he brought the bat around a little early. The next delivery was an inside fastball that crowded Luther away from the plate. The right-hander then teased the husky slugger with a curveball just off the outside corner, but Luther laid off the pitch. Harley squirmed in his seat.

Taking a short wind-up, the pitcher brought another curveball spinning toward the outside edge. Luther brought the bat around with extended arms, lining the ball over the shortstop's head. Harley was on his feet as Wilkins, Kerr, and McCoy all scored on the drive up the gap in left center. Luther lumbered all around to third base where Frank Knight was smiling and offering congratulations.

Down the aisle from Harley two fans slammed their scoreboards down in disgust. One commented dejectedly, "Two doubles, a triple, and a home run! That guy killed us! How in the world can you throw a hitter that many fat pitches in one afternoon?"

Zoltowski retired the side in order in the bottom of the ninth. Harley made his way down the left field line to the visitors' clubhouse. Along the way he overheard a number of local fans with poker player vocabularies. Luther's hitting had stirred up a hornet's nest.

Harley found George Hauser at the water cooler. The manager grinned at the owner. "Well, boss, nothing like a big finish. We had that one all the way."

The owner nodded. "I suppose you're going to tell me you planned it that way — having Barber up at the dish with bases jammed."

George rubbed his chin. "As I recall that's exactly the way I wrote the script."

Harley motioned the manager over to the small coaches' room. Inside the owner told his old friend, "Well, someone else is about to write a script, and I have a feeling we're not going to care for his comments about the main character."

It took less than three minutes to explain the situation to the veteran skipper, and another two minutes to corral Luther and bring him into the room.

When Harley mentioned the name, Paul Morran, Luther whirled on him with such force that he nearly lost his balance. "I'm not talking with that man, not tomorrow, not anytime. If he values his life, he'll stay clear of me. The man's not a legitimate sportswriter. He's nothing more than a muckraker who gets his thrills poking his nose into ball players private lives. I'm warning both of you right now; you let this bum in the clubhouse, and there's going to be bad trouble!" The brawny infielder stormed out of the room.

Later, when the bus pulled out of the parking lot and headed for Auburn, George Hauser made his way to a seat next to his first baseman. "I'm sorry about your wife, Luther. Harley heard about your loss when he talked with Greta this afternoon."

George noticed tears forming in the big man's eyes. When he started to talk, the tone of his voice was in a funeral whisper. "I really miss her. I was no prize as a husband, no one knows that better than I do, but she never complained. I should have said a lot of things to her, nice things, but I never got around to it. Then she was gone, and it was too late. A man should always take the time to thank a person like that. That guy Morran, he said I made my wife ill with some of my problems in baseball, but that was a lie, and he knew it when he stuck it in the paper. Cathy and I, we got along great. I was trying so hard to make it to the big leagues. I'd get discouraged, sometimes lose my temper, say things in public that I should have kept to myself. It never bothered her; she understood. When Morran would write that trashy stuff, she just dropped the papers in the wastebasket. She always said, 'We know differently, don't we, Luther?' The guy never bothered her in the least."

George laid his hand on the man's shoulder. "Don't be concerned about Morran. I can assure you he won't get within shouting distance of the clubhouse. If I'm wrong, and he makes it through the front gate, I'll help you throw him out. Not that you would need any help, mind you. It's just that I consider it my responsibility to keep undesirables out of that pretty little park."

Up front in the bus, Harley was taking a nap. George gave him a shake. "When you see Morran tomorrow, please inform him you have a manager that plans to throw him out the gate. You needn't mention that Luther will be helping me!"

George could hear the owner twittering beneath his hat.

CHAPTER
6

INSIDE BASEBALL

Between a dawn and a sunset, the Morran-Barber matter had put all other Burlington baseball business on the back burner. By two o'clock the next day, however, things were back to normal. Harley and Morran held a lengthy confab in the owner's office, and the Bears' boss did most of the talking.

In spite of the intervening wall, Greta could not help but hear most of the conversation. From the tone of Harley's voice she knew he was hotter than a glassblower's breath. She could hear him pounding his desk. Then she heard his words loud and clear. "If you feel up to it Morran, now's the time. Will you take it sitting, or would you prefer to stand up?"

Greta jumped up from her desk and dashed toward her boss's office. When she reached the doorway, she heard Harley say, "Care to remove your glasses?"

As Greta held her breath, Morran took his glasses off and laid them on Harley's desk.

The Bears' chief took a step forward. At that instant Morran waded in with a long swinging right. There was nothing wrong with his courage, just his technique. Harley sidestepped the right hand lead and landed a short left on the writer's chin. Morran's knees buckled, and he fell against the desk. When his head cleared, he took another swing with his right hand, but Harley ducked under the punch. The owner then landed a quick left hand into Morran's midsection. Greta could hear the wind whistle out of the writer's body, like air from a squeezed bellows. He sank to the floor. When he managed his feet, the fight was over. Grabbing his glasses, Morran hurried by Greta without comment.

The secretary turned her attention to Harley. "Boss," she exclaimed, "You were magnificent!" After a pause she could not help but ask, "Where in the world did you learn all those moves? I hope you realized that Morran just might be half your age."

Harley laughed loudly. "A man's only as old as he wants to be, Greta. When Morran called me a few nasty names, I suddenly shed twenty five years. I don't approve of settling differences in that manner, but once in awhile there's no other choice. We won't have any more trouble from Mr. Morran."

Greta smiled slyly, "You know, boss, I really feel George and Frank should hear about this. Would you like me to give them a blow by blow account of the entire bout?"

Harley's eyes brightened. "Greta, I'd appreciate that very much. In fact I wouldn't mind if your memory did a few tricks; maybe you could have me dancing around the room like Gentleman Jim Corbett — you know bobbing and weaving, landing all types of punches. I've been taking wisecracks from those two old birds for years. What an opportunity to turn the tables!"

Greta laughed softly. "I'll see what I can do. In the meantime we have a ball game to win this afternoon. The club should be about ready to take the field."

Welterroth was scheduled to go six innings for the Bears if the innings were not too difficult. Pete Gleason was to work the last three frames.

The Spring Haven Athletics solved Welterroth for two runs in the very first inning. The chunky right hander threw an easy doubleplay ball into center field, and the Athletics capitalized by making sure that both runners scored. In the third inning McCoy missed the cut-off man after playing a base hit into right field. When the throw sailed over Barber's head on the fly to Meadowcroft, the base runner easily took second base. He scored with two outs when the next hitter slashed a base hit up the middle.

When Welterroth left after the top of the sixth, the Bears had committed 3 official errors plus a couple of costly mental mistakes. George Hauser was upset.

Spring Haven had a crafty left-hander on the hill. He was staying ahead of the hitters in the count, and was using a sharp breaking curveball to great advantage. Reems and Barber were both hitless. In fact, neither had been able to get the ball out of the infield. Going into the bottom of the sixth inning, the Bears had managed only four scattered singles.

Center fielder Jack Goodman led off with a solid double into the left field corner. Catcher Hal Meadowcroft grounded out second to first, and George sent Ed Wickland up to hit for Welterroth. Ed hit a blooper into short center field that dropped for a single. The Bears now trailed 4-1. Second baseman Eddie Wilkins stroked a clean base hit between third and short, and Wickland held at second. Barney Kerr worked the left-hander for a base on balls. With the bases full the Bears had the meat part of their batting order coming up. Right fielder McCoy stepped in to hit.

McCoy worked the count to 2-2 and then laced a line-drive base hit into left field. Wickland scored easily from third, but Wilkins had to lay up at third, as the left fielder charged the ball and cut loose with a hard accurate throw to the plate.

Luther Barber got beneath a good letter-high fastball and skied it to medium deep center field. Wilkins tagged and came home after the catch. It appeared that the Bears were within one run. However, the Athletics put the ball in play at the mound, and then appealed that Wilkins left third base too quickly. Instantly the base umpire shouted, "You're Out!" George Hauser jumped from the bench and started to argue the play, but Frank Knight, coaching at third base, waved him off. Apparently Wilkins had left the bag too soon. To make matters worse, Reems took a called third strike to end the inning.

44

The seventh and eighth innings passed without either club putting a man on base. In the top of the ninth, Spring Haven pushed over two more runs. A left-hand hitting first baseman drilled a high curveball from Gleason over the right field fence. One out later, another left hand hitter drove a double into the gap in right center. He later scored on a ground single through the infield.

In the bottom of the ninth the Bears went down quietly on three easy flyballs to the outfield. George Hauser could not remember when one of his clubs had played so poorly defensively. Offensively, the work at the plate had been disappointing. He meant to mention the base running to a number of players. Tomorrow was a practice day, and he would have plenty to say.

The following morning he had all the players gathered on the grass portion of the infield. He asked them to make themselves comfortable.

"Men, I'm sure you share my concern regarding the type of baseball we played out here yesterday. To win in good competition we must play aggressive baseball. I've said countless times that no player can be too aggressive for me. We played "Caution baseball" yesterday. To me that's losing baseball. We were waiting for something nice to happen. In this game you never wait; you go out and make things happen. Hitters, fielders, base runners, and pitchers must be aggressive. Now for a few specifics." All the players felt the uneasiness of the situation. "Gleason, you were trying to be too cute with that leadoff man. Your number one priority with a leadoff man, and here I mean the number one man in any official batting order, is to make him hit the ball. You can't fool around with too many breaking pitches. Put something on the fastball and keep it in the strike zone. If you get ahead of him then of course use your breaking stuff. Be aggressive; go right after him. Now for our hitters. We took too many pitches yesterday, pitches we should have been jumping on. Again, we were too cautious at the plate." Pausing for a moment, George took up the subject of mental mistakes.

"Wilkins, you were not thinking at third base. There are times when a baserunner must get a very close jump at third base to score on a flyball. Yesterday was no such occasion. You could have waited until the ball left the outfielder's hand and still scored standing up. So why take the chance in leaving too early? I know you realize the importance of good baserunning at any time during the game, but when you have worked yourself around to third base you are only 90 feet from scoring a run. No baserunner can afford to make a mistake in that position. McCoy, you've got the best throwing arm in our outfield, but you were not thinking when you cut loose with that throw to Meadowcroft in the third inning. You threw the ball ten feet over Luther's head. How in the world can that type of throw be cut off? Luther's big enough to tilt the infield, but his arms are only a few inches longer than mine. You outfielders must keep those throws down in that type of situation. Welterroth, you were not thinking when you threw that double-play ball into center field. I know Frank here has worked with all you pitchers on that play. If the ball is hit sharply back to any of you pitchers, you must wait for a couple of seconds to allow the infielder to reach the bag, or to be near the bag. If the ball is hit slowly back to you, then, of course, you can wheel and fire the ball. Yesterday the infielder was not allowed enough time to make the play."

Frank Knight stepped into the circle to make a few comments. "While we have everyone together this morning, I want to mention the young pitcher who will be joining the club next month. For the new players on the roster this year I want to talk a few minutes about the special infield alignment which we used last season when this boy was on the mound. Joel Travis has a physical disability and cannot cover first base. George set up a different type of alignment for the infielders, and this boy turned out to be one of

46

the three best winners in the league. Luther, when we're finished here we're going to have a little infield practice using this different alignment. Joel will be finishing up his senior year of high school the second week of May. When he reports up at Burlington, he plans to be ready for a starting assignment. Once the season starts, we'll have little time to work on the new alignment. I know George wants this matter ironed out in the next few days.''

When the meeting with the players broke up, George and Frank put the regular infield to work. They had Miller playing in front of the bag whenever a bunting type of hitter might be at the plate. Luther was instructed to play in front of the bag under the same circumstances. Barney Kerr was moved a couple of steps to his right to get balls hit by Miller's left. With a non-bunter at the plate, Luther shallowed up a little at first, and Eddie Wilkins moved two big steps to his left. He was to call Luther off most balls which would force the big first baseman too far off the first base bag. On bunts Joel would be able to take the ones off the lines and within reasonable distance of the mound. Miller would have to charge quickly and take the ones down the third base line. Luther would have to do likewise with the ones down his way. Wilkins had to be there to take the first baseman's throws. Meadowcroft and Wickland proved last year that they could bounce out from behind the plate and make the plays around and in front of the plate.

George and Frank used two sets of infielders while running the drills. After forty five minutes both were satisfied that the alignment would be just as productive as it had been during the 1947 season.

While George set up some batting practice, Frank took a number of the pitchers down to the bull pen. While several loosened up, Frank centered his attention on left-hander Pete Gleason. After throwing for a few minutes, Gleason joined Frank behind the mound.

''Pete, I believe I can help you. I want you to try a

47

few things for me this morning. Number one, I want you to pitch off the first base side of the rubber. At present your left foot is more to the third base side than the first. You're having some problems getting the left-hand hitters out. Now I feel you have a better than average curveball, and that's the pitch you have to get these hitters out with. By moving toward first base on the rubber you'll have a better angle with your curveball. Also I want you to take a little speed off your curveball. At present you're throwing it much too hard. You're not allowing the break to take place. One more thing. I want you to bend your right knee a little more on your follow through. You must bend at the knees if you hope to keep your pitches down in the strike zone. I would wager that better than half your pitches yesterday were above the belt of the hitters. If we can get you down in your follow through, I believe we can eliminate some of those home runs and long flyballs to the fence. You need to produce more ground balls.''

Before Frank left the southpaw, he worked with the pitcher on one other important matter. He asked the hurler to take less time between his pitches. Frank was from the old school and believed in getting the ball from the catcher, taking your sign, and pumping in the next pitch without much delay. He never cared much for slow working pitchers.

After lunch Frank Knight took most of the pitchers over to another field just beyond Benson's playing area. Working off the mound, the pitching coach had each pitcher field a number of batted balls around the hill. Frank had Kerr and Wilkins taking throws at second base. Later on, the keystone combination left, and Luther Barber joined the drills at first base. Frank noticed that the first baseman always let the pitchers get a good look at the baseball before he made his throws to the bag. His throws were always up where the pitchers could handle them easily.

By three o'clock, Frank had everyone back on the main field. It was nearly four thirty before George called an end to the workout. Before the players left for the clubhouse, he called a short meeting on the field.

"Men, tomorrow we play Lockport here, two o'clock starting time. Everyone be dressed and ready to go by noon. I've already talked to the players I want out here in the morning for extra batting practice. From now on we'll be playing ball games every afternoon. Be sure to keep me posted on any injuries that might demand treatment or a day or two's rest. Here's the lineup for tomorrow:

> Wilkins, 2b
> Kerr, ss
> McCoy, rf
> Barber, 1b
> Reems, lf
> Miller, 3b
> Bayman, cf
> Wickland, c
> Codrington, p

As the manager walked from the field, he was joined by his pitching coach. "George, guess who might be here tomorrow for that afternoon game?"

"Can't imagine," replied the tired field boss.

"Joel Travis, that's who."

George immediately perked up. "Joey's coming down from Connersburg?"

Frank nodded.

George grabbed his coach by the arm. "How long will he be in town?"

"Probably just tomorrow. His Mother said he has a couple of days off from school. He should be at the train station shortly before noon."

George could remember the day last year when Joel reported to the Burlington spring camp. Harley, Frank, and himself had 'put a stout heart to a steep hill,' but the boy had responded just like a seasoned veteran. In all his years of managing he had never taken to a player like the youngster from Connersburg. The boy was at home reading sports pages or studying Shakespeare, Walt Whitman, and Robert

Browning. His Christian beliefs were unshakable.

The desire to help one's fellow man is the noblest refinement of elementary hunger. Joel Travis had helped each and every member of his club last year. The boy had a natural gift to inspire.

The ball club had been flat and listless of late. Joey's visit might change things around.

CHAPTER

7

JOEL TRAVIS

Every window facing east in the big farm house was opened to the garden where the flowers yielded their fragrance. Joel found his Mother in the dew drenched garden, kneeling over some small flowers that needed her special attention. Her wide brimmed straw hat had given away her position.

Towering over her, he said softly, "Mother, Corey's here, and it's time I left for the station. Is there anything I can do for you before I leave?"

"I'll be fine. Don't keep Corey waiting. It's so nice of the man to give you transportation at such an early hour." Rising slowly, she gave Joel a warm smile. "Don't forget to pass along my kindest regards to Mr. Hauser, Mr. Walsh, and, of course, to Mr. Knight. You be sure to let them know that I am feeling very well, and that we are being protected by the same Hand that looks after these fine gentlemen. Now you be off."

Joel hurried from the garden, stopping for a second at the house to pick up his small suitcase.

Before entering Corey's gray sedan, he paused to wave and shout. "I'll be back on the Monday passenger! Corey's going to be meeting the train! I should be home by noon!"

Corey Taylor headed east over the rolling, dusty county road. At forty, the Connersburg farmer was still boyish-looking, his unruly sandy hair sticking out beneath his Connersburg baseball cap. If anyone in the county followed baseball any closer than Corey, it was news to Joel. When Corey wasn't working his 80 acre red-clay farm west of Connersburg, he was reading about the baseball world or attending some ball game at the high school or county level. The only time he got side-tracked from either was when he went coon hunting with his prize Redbone black and tan hounds.

This morning Corey felt like talking. "Joey, take a good look at that Barber fella this afternoon. They had a big spread in the Burlington paper about him. After you signed last year, Florence sent in for a subscription to that paper. Just like yourself, we've been following the Bears' games down south. That fella must be a mighty fine hitter; mercy, he's been wearing those pitchers out down there."

"I'll give you a full report when I get back, Corey." Joel then added, "Barber must be terribly strong to hit those tape measure home runs. I never thought I would see anyone hit the ball harder and farther than Henry Pearce, but, then again, that's baseball, something different each and every season."

The little sedan bounced over a bumpy side street near the railroad station. Joel turned and lifted his suitcase from the back seat. Within seconds Corey had parked the car, and the two of them walked toward the depot. Inside Joel checked with the ticket master. His train was on time.

Corey was anxious to get back to work. "Joey, be careful now. No sense of me hanging around this place. Have a good trip, and I'll be here tomorrow at noon." He then turned on his heel and strode from the station.

Ten minutes later Joel had boarded his train, and in another five minutes the passenger was moving through Connersburg. He settled back in the comfortable seat and watched intently as the familiar buildings came and passed by the window.

As the train moved swiftly through the countryside, Joel could hear the shrill whistle sounding the passenger's approach to a rural crossing. If there was a more romantic and thrilling story of the nation's growth than the story of the birth of the great trains and railroads, it had escaped Joel. Like his departed father, he had always held a special love for the gargantuan giants who sped swiftly on slippers of steel to all parts of the country. He could well imagine the old steamers of the past cutting through high mountains, thundering into driving blizzards, and bridging great rivers with a full head of steam. For many people train traveling might be dull and tedious, but for himself there was no other way to complete a journey.

Joel gave thought to his teammates in Auburn. He was anxious to see them all; however, the player he had missed the most was catcher Hal Meadowcroft. He wondered what kind of spring the big receiver was having down south. The Burlington paper seldom listed spring training averages. He knew Meadowcroft would be battling Ed Wickland for the number one catching job. Both men were good receivers, but last season Meadowcroft had won the starting position with some solid stick work.

Meadowcroft was but twenty years of age and had close family ties back home in Virginia. The catcher's Mother had believed that baseball was a den of iniquity. Hal had been practically disinherited at first, but was finally forgiven. Joel felt the good natured catcher had a very promising future in professional baseball.

Joel also thought about Frank Knight. He knew that Knight was the sole reason he was in professional baseball. His admiration for the elderly gentleman was limitless. The veteran scout and coach had a quizzical humor, sincerity, and a willingness to see any player's problems and to compromise on methods but not on principles. When he had lost his father last summer, Frank Knight was the man he had turned to for solace. It had been nearly three months since the two had talked. He could hardly wait for the coming meeting.

Half through the morning the train slowed down in a small village. Joel caught a glimpse of a little wooden church, humble and old, but dignified and serene, amid its quiet surroundings. He leaned his head back and closed his eyes. When he awoke, the fast moving passenger had moved along to greener pastures and changing farm lands. That lighthearted young lady, Spring, had been industriously making beauty.

Just before the train pulled into the Auburn station, Joel pulled himself up from his coach seat and smoothed the wrinkles from his trousers. Five minutes later he was standing on the station platform. Then he heard the voice of Frank Knight.

"Joey! Over here!"

Turning, Joel picked his friend out of a small cluster of people near the main entrance to the station. When Frank grabbed his hand, he said, "Son, you look great. Land sakes, you're a sight for these tired old eyes. How's your Mother?"

"She's just fine, and sends her very best to you, Mr. Hauser, Harley, and all the players. She was working in her flower garden when I left early this morning."

"Joey, grab that suitcase of yours and we'll hurry over to the hotel. They're not going to be eating lunch at the field today, so we might as well order something at the Larchmont. Growing boy like yourself must be mighty hungry."

Shortly before noon, Joel ordered fried chicken, beans, bread, and cold tea to drink. The conversation then turned to baseball. Joel asked about the progress of the ball club.

"Too early to tell," replied the coach. "Our last game was poorly played. Too many mental mistakes, George can't take that kind of baseball; it really gnaws at his insides. You know that as well as I do, Joey." Frank continued, "We have had some bright spots, however. I believe Pete Gleason will work himself into the regular rotation. He's green, but the kid's coming on fast. He's a good listener and a hard worker. Luther Barber might be the key to our whole season. I can't remember when I've seen a hitter with better power and consistency. He has the ability to carry this club with that big bat. Joey, you wouldn't believe some of the drives that Barber's hit

54

down here. He's not just a hard swinger. He makes contact at the plate by being a smart hitter. He doesn't chase bad pitches, and he's a good breaking ball hitter. I would have to say the man is one of the best hitters that I've come across in this game, and I've seen a few, Joey."

"How come he's playing in a "AA" league?"

Frank conceded his bewilderment. "Don't ask me to explain anything about Luther Barber. Apparently the man has gone through some tough personal problems. He still carries a chip on both shoulders; you just can't get close to him. At times he melts a little, but then he hardens like a poured batch of concrete. The only player he confides in the slightest is Barney Kerr. We did find out the other day that Barber lost his wife a number of years ago. He's been a troubled man ever since. I've tried to gain his confidence, but it's like yesterday; I asked him if he was satisfied with the way things were working out down here. You know, I thought he might want to get something off his chest. Well, he just looked right through me and then walked off. He's no troublemaker, Joey, in fact he's one of the hardest working players in camp. I could really like the big lug if he gave me half a chance."

Joel gazed intently at his friend. "Maybe Luther never played for an owner like Mr. Walsh, a coach like yourself, or a manager like George Hauser. Maybe he never had teammates like he'll have on this club. Compassion has been known to do wonders."

Frank smiled, and nodded his head in total agreement. "Joel, for a young man, you've got a heap of common sense."

When their meal had been consumed, the waitress delivered the check, and Frank signed it quickly. Grabbing his hat, the Bears' coach jumped up from the table. "Come on, Joey, let's get out to the field. Boys should be starting batting practice about now. We can watch Luther drive a few over the fence."

When the two of them reached Benson Field, the Bears' players were just leaving the clubhouse. Meadowcroft spotted Joel and ran towards the young pitcher. Grabbing Joel in a bear hug, the big catcher lifted him completely off the ground and whirled him around like a trackman would whirl a discus. They laughed together. "Joey, how have you been? Looks to me like you're just about ready to go nine innings!"

"Not quite," answered Joel. "I might last three or four, but I've got a long way to go yet before I could start and finish a game. I'll be through school in a few weeks. By then I should be close to being in good shape."

Meadowcroft grinned, "Hey, roomie, just watch me drive that ball this afternoon. Pitchers down here can't get me out."

Joel laughed aloud, "Doesn't mean a thing Hal. Everybody down here knows you're strictly a spring-training hitter."

"Joey, you know better than that. Look at all those games I won for you last year. Not just with my great catching, but with that big bat of mine."

Joel winked at Frank Knight. "Give me a few minutes, Hal. I might come up with one or two."

The big catcher shook his head. "That's a buddy for you. Takes every darn thing for granted." Giving Joel a friendly push, he hurried toward the field.

Joel spent the next several minutes shaking hands and visiting with his teammates. He met the new players, including Luther Barber. The big first baseman squeezed his hand firmly, but there was no verbal greeting. Joel could hardly believe the size of the man. He had a bull's neck and shoulders, which tapered down to a medium sized waist. The first sacker's forearms could have been developed shaping horseshoes. His thigh muscles bulged beneath his uniform pants. Joel could imagine a pitcher's reaction when viewing this man standing in the batter's box.

Down in the dugout Joel met manager George

Hauser. "Son, you've made everybody's day around here. Have you been throwing every day? I want you to be ready when you report."

"I've been throwing a good half hour every afternoon at the high school field," replied Joel. "My arm feels fine; it's just a little weak, that's all. When I come up to Burlington next month I should be ready to start." He then asked about the other Bear pitchers.

"We're coming along all right, Joey. Welterroth looks to be about ready. Codrington, Wyant, and Doty are not far behind. Carl Zoltowski needs some more work. The new left-hander, Pete Gleason, keeps improving. Frank thinks the kid can work himself into being a spot starter for us. We have another young pitcher by the name of John Terrance who might make the club. I plan to use him tomorrow for two or three innings. I'd like to use him as a middle man out of the bullpen this summer."

"I guess the hitting looks good, doesn't it?"

"Joey, that looks to be our ace in the hole. At first I thought our run production would really hurt us. To win in "AA" you certainly have to produce runs. With the loss of Henry Pearce we were really hurting. Then this Barber guy shows up."

Joel nodded, "Frank told me all about him this morning."

"Well, Joey, he makes hitting look easy. He knows the mechanics of being a good hitter, and he puts them to good use. His power is unbelievable. He simply muscles the ball right out of the ball park. He's hit some balls here that must have traveled 475 feet or more." The manager laid his hand on Joel's arm. "He's taking his turn in the cage now. Just watch and you'll see some raw power."

Joel studied the burly infielder as he awaited the batting practice pitch. Barber held the bat very high and still. When the pitch came down he took a short stride into the ball and brought a black bat around with terrific force. There was a sharp crack as the ball shot high and deep into left center field. Players

57

shagging in the outfield barely moved. The ball disappeared at the 385 mark. Joel looked back to George Hauser. "See what I mean?" The manager shook his head slowly.

Shortly before game time, Joel left the dugout for a seat behind home plate. When he had settled himself behind the screen, he took note of the Lockport pitcher warming up in front of the first base dugout. The right-hander could throw hard, but his curveball was lazy and lacked power.

In front of the third base dugout, Codrington was loosening up. The veteran right-hander was a manager's pitcher. He always got the ball over the plate with something on all of his pitches. He was a good student of pitching. Joel had learned a great deal from his pitching teammate last season.

At two o'clock sharp the Bears took the field.

In the top of the first Codrington retired the first three hitters easily. The right-hander for Lockport was just as effective getting Wilkins and Kerr on groundballs, and striking out McCoy on a good inside fastball.

Codrington registered two strikeouts in the top of the second. The other hitter popped behind the plate to Meadowcroft. Joel awaited Barber's appearance at the batter's box.

The right-hander for Lockport fired a good fastball over the outside corner for a called strike. He came back with a good change off the fastball, and Luther fouled the pitch down the left field line. The next three pitches were fastballs that crowded the hitter. Barber fouled them back to the screen. The following pitch was a fastball that Joel thought was a little inside, just missing the corner. However, the plate umpire saw it differently. His right hand came up, and he shouted, "You're out!"

Joel watched Barber's reaction carefully. He was sure the big man would argue the call, but he only switched his bat to his left hand and walked slowly back to the dugout. Stuart Reems flied to medium-deep left center for the second out. Chet Miller ended the inning with a pop to the Lockport third sacker.

The game was moving along in a hurry. Codrington and the Lockport right-hander were both throwing no-hitters through the fifth inning. Barber had been the only base runner in the game, drawing a walk leading off in the fifth. Both clubs had made several nice plays in the field.

In the seventh the action picked up, Lockport started to get to Codrington. The Bears right-hander was starting to lose a little velocity off his fastball. With one out, the Lockport catcher caught a middle-of-the-plate fastball and drove it well over the left field fence. After a single between short and third, the third baseman for Lockport hit a line drive up the alley in left center. Before Bayman could retrieve the ball, the speedy infielder was standing at third base. Codrington got the next hitter on a flyball to McCoy, but the runner at third tagged up and scored easily. When the next hitter had grounded out to end the inning, Codrington walked slowly to the dugout. Joel felt the right-hander had pitched very well for this early in the season. He simply had ran out of gas.

Barney Kerr led off the seventh for the Bears. The little shortstop pushed a bunt between the mound and first base. Joel could see that the play at the bag was going to be very close. The umpire hesitated for just a second and then called Kerr out. The Burlington infielder was furious. He charged back at the umpire, placing his body directly in front of the arbitrator. Joel could hear the infielder's words. ''I had the throw beat! You know I had it beat! You can't take a base hit away from me just because the guy's got a no-hitter going!'' The umpire listened for a few seconds, and then walked away down the right field line.

McCoy, the next Bears' hitter, worked the count to 3-2. The Lockport hurler tried a fastball at the knees, but the pitch dipped below the strike zone.

Joel leaned a little forward in his seat as Luther Barber left the on-deck circle. After looking at third

base coach Frank Knight for his sign, Barber dug in at the plate.

Joel noted that the pitching pattern for Barber in this game seemed to be to keep the fastball in on his hands.

The first delivery was a curveball that missed the outside corner. The next pitch was a fastball on the inside corner, and the husky first baseman must have been looking for just such a pitch. With the quickness of a big cat, he opened up his hips and brought the bat around. Joel had never seen a ball hit so hard. Just beyond the left-field fence there was a good sized brick building which was used for housing field maintenance equipment. Barber's drive cleared the roof of the building with plenty to spare. Joel rubbed his eyes in disbelief.

Luther circled the bases with his head down. Frank Knight shook his hand as he rounded third.

Most of the Bear players were at the plate to offer congratulations.

After Barber's clout, the right-hander for Lockport had trouble finding the strike zone. He walked Stuart Reems and Chet Miller on eight pitches. Phil Bayman slapped a single through the middle, and Reems scored the tying run. With runners on first and third, Hal Meadowcroft walked to the plate. Joel shouted some encouragement to his last season's roommate.

The Lockport manager walked to the mound and called in another right-hander from the bullpen. When action resumed, Joel again leaned forward in his seat. Meadowcroft took his stance in the batter's box.

Sometimes it seems the ball has eyes for a hungry hitter, and this is what happened to the batted ball that Meadowcroft stroked. It wasn't hit hard, but it was placed half way between the shortstop and the third baseman. Both infielders missed reaching the ball by a couple of inches. Miller came home with the go ahead run. Don Carruthers hit for Codrington and bounced into a fast double play ending the inning.

Tom Wyant worked the last two innings for Burlington, and the seasoned veteran faced only six men. The Bears had a well earned 4-3 victory.

In the clubhouse Joel made the rounds congratulating all his teammates. He stopped in front of Luther Barber's locker and caught the infielder just before he headed for the showerroom. "Luther, do you mind if I ask you a question about your home run?"

"I don't mind." was the quick reply.

"Well, I was sitting in the stands behind the plate, and I noticed that you changed your stance just a little from the two previous trips to the batter's box. It seemed to me that while the pitcher was in his wind-up to give you that fastball which you hit for your homer, you moved both of your feet a little away from the plate. Am I imagining things, or did you actually make that change?"

61

Luther stared at the young pitcher for several moments. When he spoke, his voice was light and friendly. "How old are you, Travis?"

"I'm eighteen," came the reply.

"Well, for eighteen you've got plenty of smarts. Sure I moved a few inches backward on that pitch. I couldn't give the change away to the catcher before he gave the sign, so I waited until the pitcher started his motion. I figured after that outside curveball he would come inside with another fastball." Luther grabbed his towel, "You don't miss much about this game, do you, Travis?"

"No, sir. I make it a habit to study all the hitters, even our own. Knowing how a hitter can handle a certain pitch from a certain stance is mighty important. At least to me it is."

Luther started for the showerroom. After taking a few steps, he turned and said, "Pitching's half head work. I don't know a thing about your arm, but there's nothing wrong with your thinking. I never saw an eighteen year old pitcher talk like you do. Maybe it's right that we're on the same club. You on the mound and me at the plate might be a stand off, you know." He then lumbered off down the narrow aisle toward the showers.

Joel remembered what Frank had said earlier about Luther. "I could really like the big lug if he gave me half a chance."

CHAPTER

8

WHAT WE'RE REALLY UP AGAINST

The early spring evening was flawless in warmth and blueness; there were no clouds in the wide, clear sky; the little lake was a gentle heaving piece of blue satin. Joel seated himself on a worn, wooden bench, that afforded one a beautiful view of the water and shoreline. Tomorrow morning he would be catching the train back up north to Connersburg. He knew this spot well, for last year in spring training he had visited the lake many times to relax and gather his thoughts. This evening he had brought along a copy of Hamlin Garland's book "Back Trailers from the Middle Border." Ever since he had read Garland's "A Son of the Middle Border," the urge had been present to read everything the Wisconsin native had put to print. Garland wrote about the land, about farming, and the plight of the early midwestern farmers.

After reading for nearly an hour, Joel laid the book aside and took a small knife from his pocket. He picked up a small, weathered piece of wood and whittled a few slivers from its surface.

"Thinking about home?"

The closeness of the voice startled Joel. Looking around, he saw the tall form of Luther Barber.

"I guess maybe I was, just a little."

The muscular older man lowered his body to the wooden bench. "Sort of peaceful down here, isn't it?"

Joel nodded, "Last spring I spent a good many hours down here. With my trying to make the club and all, it just seemed I needed some place where I could sit and think things through. We've got a place back home that comes mighty close to this view. On certain days the sky is almost as brightly tinted as the deep blue waters of the lake.''

Luther picked up the Garland book. ''Like to read, Joel?''

''Yes, sir.''

The big man opened the book and thumbed through a few pages.

''Live on a farm up north?''

''Yes, sir. My Mother and I have a place with a big farm house and over a hundred acres about 300 miles north of here.''

Luther laid the book aside. ''When I was a kid my dad bought a small farm out west. Plenty of farmers in those days lost the hard work of a whole year by an evil change in the weather. No poker-faced gambler ever took his losses with more outward serenity than those farmers. They never whined; they just pulled in their belts and waited for another planting season. I guess that's what you would call true courage and patience.''

Joel nodded in agreement.

After several minutes of complete silence, Luther asked, ''What else do you like to read?''

''Oh I enjoy reading just about anything about baseball, music, trains; and I like reading the classics.''

''The Bible?''

Joel turned his head sharply and studied the man's face. Luther sat with his head bowed slightly.

''The Bible best of all,'' replied Joel. Then in a soft voice he asked, ''Why did you ask me that?''

Luther raised his head and smiled slightly. ''The other day I was talking with your old friend, Frank Knight. Knight seems to know a great deal about his ball players. You're no exception. He mentioned your spiritual integrity.''

Before Joel could say what was on his mind, Luther reached over and gently removed the small

64

knife from his hand. "Young man, do you realize that the word "Penknife" is one of the words found only once in the Bible?"

Joel finally found his voice. "No, sir, I never realized that."

Folding the blade into the case, he added, "Did you realize that the capital letter "Q" can be found but twice in the Old Testament and three times in the New?"

Again Joel searched for his voice. When he answered, he tried hard to say his words clearly. "No, sir, I never realized that either."

The burly athlete laughed aloud, and with a light tone to his voice said, "You see, I've managed to read a little myself!"

It was nearly ten minutes later when the conversation was renewed. "Do you and your Mother enjoy music, Joey?"

"Mother plays the piano, and I'm always teasing her to play some of the old time songs for me."

Luther's eyes brightened. "Seems as though our Mothers had a great deal in common."

A few minutes later Joel tried to find out a bit more about the infielder's personal life, but the attempt failed miserably. Luther cut him off abruptly.

"I've enjoyed visiting with you, Travis, but it's time I moved along." His voice had turned hard and rather coarse. "Have a safe trip back home. If I'm still with the club next month, I'll see you up in Burlington." He walked away without another word.

Joel waited for the last sounds of Luther's retreat to die away. He wished he had not tried to bring the man out of his darkened shell. Luther, as yet, was not ready to let any person pry into his private life. Joel had no wish to dig into the man's personal life; it was just that he knew the spirit of cooperation was a necessity for any winning ball club. When all the individuals were merged into one harmonious whole, then, and only then, could a ball club play inspired baseball.

As Joel walked slowly back to the hotel, he thought about Luther's last statement; "If I'm still with the club next month, I'll see you up in Burlington." What was that suppose to mean? Was he thinking about leaving the ball club? Did he foresee some sort of trouble that would jeopardize his position with the Bears?

Inside the Larchmont Joel found Harley Walsh buying a few cigars and joking with the man behind the counter. When the conversation had ended, he asked if he might have a few words with the owner.

"Of course, Joey. Let's grab a seat over there at the far end of the lobby." With a twinkle in his eyes he added, "There's a rumor going around that I smoke the strongest cigars in the building. Maybe even the smelliest. Have to be careful where I light these things up."

As Joel sank down into the comfortable chair, the lobby clock ticked around to nine, and it seemed everybody suddenly was silent as though by signal.

Joel asked, "Mr. Walsh, can I ask you a question about Luther Barber?"

The owner smiled, "Fire away."

"I just had a conversation with him over in the park. It just seems that he's playing baseball on a day to day basis. I mean, he talks as if he might not be around later on. Isn't there something we can do to make him feel as though he's wanted on the ball club?"

Harley lit his cigar and took a couple of quick puffs. "Joey, we've done a great deal to make Luther feel at home, but sometimes a man has to work out his own problems. I'm not a betting man, but if I were, I would wager this ball club that Luther's going to climb his mountain before the season's over. He's scratching and clawing right now, sort of picking the right spot to start his ascent. We're going to be here if he needs some help."

Joel jumped up from his chair.

"That's exactly what I wanted to hear. I'm going back home tomorrow, and I'm not going to worry about Luther at all. He's going to be up at Burlington when I get there, and he's going to be half way up his mountain. Luther's never been around folks like we've got on this club."

Harley stood up. "Couldn't have said it better myself, my boy. Now you better get upstairs and get some rest. That 7:15 A.M. passenger has a habit of leaving this place on time."

2

During the next two weeks manager George Hauser took a good look at all his ball players. When the final cut was made, he had added five new players to the 1948 roster. In addition to Pete Gleason, the left-hander from Hanover, the club added the names of right-hand pitcher John Terrance, outfielder Phil Bayman, catcher Ned Rowland, and of course, infielder Luther Barber. The club had passed through spring training with no serious injuries. Jim Doty had a stiff shoulder which was not considered serious, and Chet Miller had a jammed thumb that was responding to treatment.

Burlington would be opening the regular season on the road at Wheelersburg. After a three game series with the Miners, the club would journey to Bainbridge for three more games. On an off day they would then come home and open the next afternoon against the New London Blues. Until Doty was ready and Joel reported, George planned to use Codrington, Welterroth, Wyant, and Gleason in the regular starting rotation. Terrance and Zoltowski would head up the bullpen. He would use Doty in spot situations until his shoulder straightened out.

The regular Burlington infield would be Miller at third, Kerr at short, Wilkins at second, and Barber at first. Meadowcroft would be the first string catcher, backed up by Ed Wickland. Young Ned Rowland would be a handy man to have around. The youngster could catch in a pinch, plus do an adequate job in the infield.

The outfield was set with Stuart Reems in left, Jack Goodman in center, and McCoy in right. Ken

Lambert was capable of filling in for any of the three.

George knew that he was a fortunate manager to have such versatility among his ball players. Most of them could play two or three different positions. He even had pitchers that were capable of playing first base or in the outfield. Wyant, in fact, could be used for pinch hitting chores.

Team speed was good, with Wilkins and Kerr batting in the number one and two positions. Goodman and McCoy were both good base runners with base stealing potential. Along with Kerr and Wilkins, the two outfielders gave George a chance to hit and run, and run and hit.

With Barber in the lineup the club had better than average power. Reems, Miller, and Meadowcroft had good home run power. George was looking for maybe 50 home runs from those three. What Barber would do was anyone's guess. If he could hit 25, the club run production would certainly be a factor in the drive for the first division.

If the pitching staff could hold its own until Joel reported, George figured his club might really surprise some people. If they started badly in the Atlantic League it would be difficult to convince the players that they were not over matched.

Frank Knight had warned him about the caliber of pitching in the "AA" league. Last season in the "A" Central League they had seldom seen a staff with more than two outstanding pitchers. This year the depth on the opposing staffs would be a much different story. George knew he had to have consistent hitting to win in the long haul. Maybe his hitters would be in over their heads? What then? His mind kept coming back to Luther Barber. Would the big first baseman be willing to share some of his hitting theories with his teammates? Would he be willing to work with a teammate caught in the doldrums of a prolonged slump? If the spring training season was an accurate forecasting instrument, George was not overly enthusiastic about the final outcome. Barber would seldom speak to any of the players, let alone help them with any problems they might have on the field. He ate his meals alone and roomed alone. Several of the players had gone out of their way to visit with the man, but it's rather difficult to carry on a conversation with but one person doing the talking. After a few tries, the players threw in the towel.

On the afternoon before departing spring training, George called a meeting of the club personnel. The get-together was held in the clubhouse, and George invited Harley and Greta Crim. Frank Knight started with a few comments about the pitchers and then turned things over to the Bears' manager.

George glanced around the room. His players sat quietly before their lockers. As in the past they planned to give him their utmost attention.

"Men, day after tomorrow we start playing for keeps. We start play in the Atlantic League with a single game at Wheelersburg. I'm not sure we can handle "AA" baseball, but I know one manager in this room who has to be shown that we're just a class "A" ball club. For the benefit of the new players I'd like to say a word about the fans we have in Burlington. They're the best in baseball, as far as I'm concerned. Oh, they'll get on your hides when you play like amateurs; I can promise you that. But it's only because they want you to do better. It's because they know you have the talent or you wouldn't have that uniform on. If we play good solid baseball, we can fill that ball park every single home date."

George paused for a moment and held up a copy of the 1948 Bears' roster. "Every player in this room has earned a place on this ball club. In my judgment we have a club with much more depth than what we had in Burlington last year. The pitching staff might be a little thin until Joey reports, but every department is deep in talent and numbers. It's very important that we get off to a running start. Playing catch-up in our situation will be no picnic, believe me. Down here we've been scoring runs. We've faced a few good pitchers, but up north we're going to be facing a good stuff pitcher practically every time out. You hitters will have to be aggressive, yet selective at the plate in this league. You must be aggressive with the pitches you can handle. When you get your pitch, jump on it. I know we'll be facing a good many pitchers who like to nibble around the strike zone, pitchers who know how to pitch with outstanding control. If you start chasing that type of pitching, you're in deep trouble. Once you're labeled a bad ball hitter, you'll never get a good pitch to hit."

The manager pointed to owner Harley Walsh. "I've been one of the more fortunate managers in this game. I've had this man for a boss for more years than most of you players have been playing this game. If you have a problem, a non baseball problem let's say, that doesn't fall under my jurisdiction, go see this man. I can personally guarantee that his door will always be wide open. He's always been a ball player's owner."

George paused to put some added expression into his parting remarks. "In closing I want to thank each of you for your efforts down here this spring. My players have always been able to play good hard baseball because they always leave spring training in top physical condition. My players have been able to think under pressure because they work hard to keep their minds on the game. My players have a sense of fair play, sportsmanship, anything you wish to call it, because they have a good moral attitude on and off the field. If we play as a team, we will all win as individuals."

Loud applause broke out throughout the room. Greta Crim dabbed at her eyes with a small pink handkerchief.

CHAPTER
9

ATLANTIC LEAGUE

The great day broke cool and clear. By noon the Wheelersburg ball park was half filled with Miner fans. Opening day meant capacity crowds for all the home clubs in the Atlantic League. On this afternoon, in addition to the Burlington-Wheelersburg game, Tyler City would be hosting Teal City; New London was visiting Pottstown; LaSalle had the home advantage over Bainbridge.

On the Bears' bench the players were about ready to take the field for batting practice. When George Hauser yelled, "Let's go!" the players scrambled from the dugout, most taking their places either in the outfield or infield. Several of the regulars headed for the batting cage.

When little Eddie Wilkins stepped in to hit, he could not help but remember what his manager, George Hauser, had told him about what type of hitter he must be to make it in pro baseball. Hauser had said, "Eddie, you probably will never weigh over 160 pounds during your baseball playing years. You're never going to be a power hitter. I want you to work on hitting the ball firmly and on the ground. Don't try for distance in the air. Get yourself a bat you can handle, and don't overswing. You're going to get a great many fastballs to hit in the leadoff position. Make sure you make the pitchers bring the ball down to you in the strike zone. High fastballs, more than not, mean pop-ups. With your speed you need to hit a number of ground balls."

Eddie got comfortable in the batter's box, then ripped a hard grounder through the right side of the infield. The next pitch was away on the outside corner, and he took a shot to left field. The result was a line drive which rolled down into the corner. He felt good today.

When the Bears had completed their batting practice, the Wheelersburg club took their infield. Chet Miller sat quietly at the end of the bench. In a few short minutes he would be up loosening the kinks out of his arm. He thought about third base and the years he had worked to master his position. His father had been a third baseman in his playing days and had shown him all the basic moves at the "Hot Corner." His father had taught him how to use his feet, how to get in front of the ball, and how to keep the ball in play at all times. He stressed the importance of always throwing the ball overhand, except when charging a bunt or slow hit ball toward the plate. The two of them had measured off the distance from the normal fielding position at third base to the first base bag. Then for hours his father had hit him ground balls, and he tossed the balls so accurately to first base that he thought he could do it blindfolded.

Miller grabbed his glove and paired up with Luther Barber. After throwing the ball back and forth a few times at fifty feet, they moved back to ninety and increased the velocity of their throws. Both concentrated on throwing the ball to the other man's letters.

The Bears took the field for infield, and George hit to the outfielders. Left-fielder Stuart Reems gunned his first throw into Eddie Wilkins at the second base bag. After another couple of throws to second and third, Reems charged a ground ball and fired it toward home plate. The ball was thrown straight overhand, across the seams, and took one long skip into Hal Meadowcroft's big mitt. The throw had been low enough to cut off if Miller so desired. If a Bears outfielder looped the ball over a cut-out man's head, he was sure to hear from George Hauser.

After a couple of rounds of fast infield, the Bears

retired to the dugout. After a few minutes of pregame ceremonies the Wheelersburg club took the field. A lean and broad-shouldered right-hander made his way to the mound. Eddie Wilkins watched the pitcher's warmups from a position to the right of the batter's box. The catcher's throw went down to second, around the horn, and back to the mound. The umpire behind the plate yelled, "Play Ball," and pulled on his mask.

The Bears second baseman took a comfortable stance in the box and leveled his bat over the plate. The right-hander took a deep breath and looked for his sign. He then swung into a big windup and brought the pitch toward the home plate. The rising fastball picked up the strike zone at the letters. Eddie took it for a called strike. A roar of approval went up from the stands. On the next delivery, Eddie drove a hard hit ground ball in the hole between short and third. The Miners shortstop moved quickly to his right, picked off the ball, set his right leg firmly, and gunned it across the infield. Eddie, running hard all the way, was retired by half a step. The Miners shortstop had a big league arm.

Barney Kerr got under a good fastball and flied out to medium depth center field. McCoy bounced out third to first. The Bears moved quickly out to their defensive positions. Codrington pulled off his jacket and stopped at the water cooler for a quick sip of water before walking slowly to the mound.

After his warmups the Bears hurler had a short talk with catcher Hal Meadowcroft. When the receiver returned to the plate, he shouted to the defensive unit, "All right now! Let's go gett'em!" A steady stream of chatter sprang up around the infield.

Codrington had little trouble with the first two Wheelersburg hitters, but the number three man doubled down the left field line. Only quick fielding by Stuart Reems held the drive to two bases. The clean-up man stepped in for the Miners. Meadowcroft went out to the mound.

Codrington started the conversation. "Let's face it, Hal, we've never seen any of these hitters. The first time around all we can do is keep the ball down and hope for the best. Let's see if we can get ahead of this guy, and then make him hit a breaking ball."

Meadowcroft nodded, and then added, "If we get behind in the count, don't give him anything fat. We've got first base open."

The Bears right-hander tried to pick up the inside corner with his first fastball, but the ball ran inside for a ball. He then missed with a curveball at the knees. Taking his stretch, he then picked up a called strike with a good breaking ball over the outside corner. Working slowly, Codrington fired a fastball for the inside portion of the plate. The big right-hand hitter took a good cut and made contact, but he didn't get the big part of the bat on the pitch. Jack Goodman made the catch in rather deep center field. Codrington breathed a sigh of relief and walked to the dugout.

At the bat rack, Barney Kerr had a few words for Luther Barber.

"Luther, this guy has a good rising fastball. He threw me one up in the letters and it really had a hop on it. His breaking ball looks to be only average. I think he'll go to his fastball when he gets behind or in trouble."

Luther nodded his head slightly, but said nothing.

As Luther stepped in to hit, Frank Knight's high voice rang out from the third base coaching box. "Come on, big fella! Get us started!"

The first pitch was a good fastball at the knees, and Luther took the pitch for a called strike. "Now you're ready! Now you're ready!" shouted George from the dugout.

The second delivery was another fastball that sailed toward the outside corner. Luther did not try to pull the fast-moving pitch. Instead he went with the offering and drove it hard into right center field. The ball took one long hop and hit the fence at the 380 mark. Luther chugged into second base with a

74

stand up double.

As Stuart Reems approached the batter's box, Frank Knight yelled out to Luther. "Nobody out now. Watch the ground ball on this side!"

Stuart Reems wanted a pitch that he could hit to right field. His job was to move Barber over to third. After taking a strike, Reems got a pitch he could handle and drove a deep flyball into right center field. Luther tagged and headed for third. The right fielder uncorked a good strong throw, and the play was close. Luther went in head first on the plate side of the bag. He chose that route because the throw came in to the outfield side of third base. Luther grabbed the bag with his right hand just before the third baseman applied the tag. For a big man it had been a daring bit of base running.

Chet Miller rubbed the batters' rosin bag on the handle of his big bat and took his sign from Frank Knight. Luther took a short lead from third.

On the first pitch Miller hit a high bouncer over the pitcher's head. Without the slightest hesitation Luther broke for the plate. The shortstop grabbed the ball and fired it to the Wheelersburg catcher. The ball arrived a second before the runner, and the hefty catcher partially blocked the plate. Luther came in at full speed with a good, clean, hard slide. The receiver's forearms were pounded with the force of Luther's driving legs. The umpire waited to make his call. The safe sign was given when the ball squirted out from beneath the two players. Miller hurried on down to second base.

When the Bears first baseman reached the dugout, he was nearly exhausted. The dashes between second and third, and third and home, had just about winded the aged infielder. Infield dirt clung to the sweaty uniform. Several of the players, plus George Hauser, came down the bench to offer congratulations. The husky slugger sat with his head in his hands between his knees, breathing heavily.

Jack Goodman lined out to left field, but Hal Meadowcroft brought Chet Miller home with a sharp single up the middle. Codrington fanned to end the inning.

Although the Miners threatened in three of the next four frames, Codrington managed to keep the home club off the scoreboard. Heading into the top of the seventh, the Bears held their 2-0 lead. The Miners right-hander had been tough in the clutch and showed no signs of weakening. In the seventh he fanned Meadowcroft and got Codrington and Wilkins on easy ground balls to the right side of the infield.

When the Miners home half of the seventh started, George got Zoltowski up in the bull pen. Codrington had already pitched more innings at one stretch than he had experienced all spring.

After sitting down from their seventh inning stretch, the home fans started the hand clapping and loud shouts to stimulate some spirit into the Miner's offense.

After retiring the first hitter on a high pop to Meadowcroft, Codrington gave up a ringing double to the Miners clean-up man. When the next hitter shot a single through the middle sending the runner across with Wheelersburg's first run, George walked slowly out to the mound.

"Getting a little tired, Joe?"

The veteran pitcher took off his cap and mopped his forehead with the right sleeve of his sweatshirt. "Maybe a little, Skip, but I'd like to stay in a little while longer."

After a moment's hesitation the manager said, "All right, let's see what you can do with this next guy. If he gets on, we'll bring Zolty in. Reach back and give him everything you've got left." Codrington nodded and returned to the rubber. George took a few steps toward the baseline and then returned. "Remember that's the tying run at first. He might be going. Throw over there a couple of times." Again Codrington nodded in agreement.

The man in the batter's box was a slim left-hand hitter. So far the Bears right-hander had been able to keep him off the bases. Meadowcroft flashed the curveball sign. Codrington took his stretch and then fired a quick throw to first base. The baserunner scrambled back head-first. When Codrington received the ball from Luther he went to the rosin bag and then stepped toward the rubber. Taking his sign, he then stretched and bent a hook toward the inside portion of the plate. The hitter slashed a mean looking ground ball toward the right field corner. For just a second Codrington's shoulders slumped, but then, with the instinct of a good fielding pitcher, he started toward first base. Luther Barber, of course, had been holding the baserunner on and had moved a couple of steps off the bag when Codrington delivered his pitch. Leaving his feet, the big first sacker made a frantic dive at the hard hit ball. Knocking the grounder down, he then scrambled to his feet and chased the ball down in foul territory. Codrington was on his way to the bag, and Luther underhanded the ball to the pitcher while on his knees. It seemed the baserunner and the Bears hurler reached the bag at exactly the same moment, but the base umpire called the runner out with a big overhand motion of his right arm. There was an immediate reaction from the first base coach for the Miners, but as is the case with all judgment calls by umpires, the argument was useless.

With a baserunner on second, Codrington worked hard on the next Miner hitter. Putting everything he had on a fastball, the Bears pitcher got the man on a high flyball to Goodman in center field.

The Bears' offense could do nothing in the top of the eighth. Codrington gave up a single in the bottom half of the inning, but pitched out of trouble. The opener was down to the last inning, and Burlington clung to a narrow one-run margin.

With two out in the ninth, Jack Goodman lined a fastball up the alley in left center field. The speedy Bears outfielder legged it all around to third base before the ball was back in the infield. Hal Meadowcroft hit another fastball right on the button, but the Wheelersburg center fielder made a nice running catch in deep left center. The big receiver was talking to himself as he strapped on his catching equipment for the last half inning.

In the Bears' bull pen Zoltowski had been joined by John Terrance. As Codrington readied to pitch, both relievers stepped up the velocity of their warmup pitches. George and Frank were up on the front step of the dugout.

With the rhythmic clapping echoing throughout the park, Codrington bent forward to take his first sign. The opening pitch of the inning was a sharp breaking curveball that cut across the outside corner for a called strike. On the next delivery the hitter drove a fastball to deep center field, but Jack Goodman retreated quickly and made the catch easily. The following Wheelersburg hitter pulled a breaking pitch down to Chet Miller at third base, and the Bears infielder retired the runner by two full steps. Some of the large crowd started making their way to the exits.

Eddie Wilkins could be heard above the other voices in the infield, "Come on, Joe! We've got the lead! One more out! That's all we need!"

Wheelersburg sent up a pinch-hitter by the name of Pendergast. Codrington, feeling the man might be a little stiff coming off the bench, went right after him with a good high velocity fastball. The hitter swung late and popped the pitch up near the first base coaching box. Luther gathered it in for the final out of the ball game.

Joe Codrington rushed over to the burly first baseman and extended his right hand. A wide smile illuminated his face. In a clear bell-like voice he said, "Luther, you saved my skin with that play at first base in the seventh inning. It kept me in the game; without it I was gone."

Barber's face contained no expression that would indicate his present mood. He merely squeezed the pitcher's hand and shuffled off toward the clubhouse.

CHAPTER

10

HITTING PROBLEMS

Harley Walsh folded his raincoat over his arm, cut an exact pipe load from a twist of tobacco, and then tamped the leaves into his briar. Just to the left of his box seat he could hear Barney Kerr in the Bears' dugout. Kerr, on this, an off day, was speaking to a group of kids from the Burlington area. The shortstop's voice cut through the early morning air, "To help you play your best defensive baseball, your glove must be thoroughly broken in. It must feel comfortable on your hand. For a shortstop or a second baseman the fingers must be short on the glove, and the surface must be smaller than that of gloves for other positions. After the glove has been carefully softened and creased, it should then be ready to help improve your fielding skill."

Harley's thoughts were not about proper defensive equipment. The ball club had hit the skids of late, and the reason for the decline was the inability of the hitters to snap out of a prolonged batting slump. The season was now entering its fifth week of competition, and the Bears had managed only an 11-20 record. The pitching had been strong enough for a first division ball club, but the Burlington hitters had produced only 65 runs in the 31 games. At first only McCoy and Miller had problems. Then Meadowcroft, Wilkins, and Reems joined the slump. Jack Goodman was starting to slide down from a fast start, and Kerr was only a few points over 260. Bayman and Lambert had been hitting well in reserve roles, and George was about ready to play them on a regular basis. The one player in the regular lineup who had not failed to live up to expectations was Luther Barber. Playing in 30 of the 31 games of the young season, Barber had recorded 9 doubles, 2 triples, and 10 home runs. He had accomplished the total bases despite being pitched around by several clubs. With Stuart Reems batting behind the big slugger, many managers were thinking twice about pitching to Barber. When Reems slumped, George moved Chet Miller up to the 5th spot in the lineup, but Miller had also failed in the back up role. It was obvious to the entire ball club that, unless several of the players snapped out of their slumps, there would be no improvement in the team standings. Opposing pitchers would be giving Luther a great many base on balls.

Through the morning hours George ran through several batting practice pitchers. He had rounded up several local sandlot hurlers to serve up pitches to his slump-ridden hitters. After lunch he again sent the local throwers to the mound and went through three more rounds of hitting. By four o'clock he was satisfied that his problem hitters had looked at enough thrown balls for one day. He could only surmise what the workout would produce. Sometimes added batting practice brought results. On the other hand, he could remember numerous times when extra work in the batter's cage seemed to hinder rather than help a bunch of frustrated hitters. Nevertheless, it had to be tried.

On Tuesday the club journeyed to Tyler City for a three game set. George named Tom Wyant to pitch the 8 P.M. encounter. Wyant had been pitching well, but like most of the Bears hurlers, he had recorded a losing record. His earned-run average stood at a respectable 3.20, but his won-lost log was a disappointing 2-4.

Tyler City started a small left-hander by the name of Charley Brumwich. Although Brumwich sounded nothing like Feller, you would have thought that the Bears hitters had mistaken him for the fire-baller from Cleveland. Through the first seven innings Burlington had managed only four hits, and all were singles. Barber had been walked twice. Wyant had pitched well but trailed 2-0.

In the eighth and ninth innings Burlington got a double from Jack Goodman and a single from Ken Lambert, but both were left stranded. In the end Tyler City won 3-0 with Brumwich recording his first victory of the season.

George Hauser knew he had to come up with some sort of solution in a hurry. Already the club was 8 games out of the top spot in the standings. Another week or ten days of this type of playing and the club could kiss a first division berth away. He was mad inside, for he knew the hitters were much better than their performances had shown. The pitching in the new league had been good, but not that good.

In his hotel room the Burlington manager pondered the situation. He had one more idea that might produce a change-around in his club's performance. The idea had more stumbling points than a walk through a strange woods at midnight, but it was all the hope he had left. Grabbing his suit coat, he quickly slipped it on and made his way from the room. He then headed for Luther Barber's room on the third floor.

Shortly after knocking upon the door of the first baseman's quarters, George heard the coarse voice of Luther Barber. "Who is it?"

George answered immediately. "It's Hauser."

The manager could hear the sound of someone getting off a bed, and then the door opened.

Luther Barber was fully dressed, and he carried a newspaper in his right hand.

"Can I talk with you a few minutes?" asked the manager.

The Bears infielder pulled the door fully open and motioned George inside. He then tossed the paper aside and took a seat on the edge of the bed.

George pulled out a chair from a small desk and seated himself in front of the muscular slugger.

"Luther, the management and the operation of this ball club is in serious trouble. As a club our hitters are a defeated lot. They have pretty much convinced themselves that this league is more than they can handle. Most of them are pressing; some I believe are so mixed up from trying everything imaginable that they have completely forgotten what type of hitters they were before the season started.''

George paused for a moment and then continued. "I've talked to each of these troubled players, and I've tried to help them to the best of my ability. To a player they've listened, and they've tried what I've suggested. I know some of the players will come out of this on their own, but going that route can be a mighty slow process. I don't have that kind of time. We need to start scoring some runs now. If we get mired down in last place, the red ink will put Harley out of business. He spent a great deal of his reserve cash to enter this league, and, so help me, somehow we've got to start winning to get those people back in the park.''

Luther looked at George as if he were a stranger. When he spoke, the tone of his voice was one of disinterest. "So what does all this have to do with me? I'm hitting the ball just like I said I would. I can't swing the bat for those other guys!''

George nodded in agreement. "No, Luther, you can't hit for your teammates. But you can help them; help them by getting up in front of each and every player and explain your theories on hitting. Tell them why they're not hitting. Don't pull any punches; lay it right on the line. Have you ever noticed how they study your hitting style in batting practice and under game conditions? They respect your hitting ability, Luther. They need help, and I can assure you, Luther, they'll listen. Those team-mates of yours will hang on your every word. Every single one will try whatever you suggest.''

Luther laughed loudly, "You're all mixed up, Hauser. Those guys could care less what I think about hitting. Half of them wouldn't even show up for such a meeting. The other half would be there to give me a rough time!''

George answered very calmly. **"You're dead** wrong, Luther. If you really believe that, you've misjudged the men on this ball club. You apparently have been hanging around with the wrong class of people. I think it's about time you gave your teammates a chance to prove themselves. Every man's entitled to a fair chance to show his sincerity on any issue, or about any person in this country. Are you going to keep your fellow players from having that chance?"

Luther studied the veteran manager; his eyes stared at the older man. At last he shifted his gaze to another part of the room. Standing up abruptly, he then walked to a point in front of a half opened window. For several seconds he said nothing, then turning he said in a hoarse growl, "I didn't sign into this outfit to be any hitting instructor. But I'm not as low down as a lot of people around here think I am. I'll talk at your meeting, but the first time one of those rookies pops off at me, the meeting's over. I can help most of them if they'll listen!"

George jumped up from his chair and started for the door. With one hand on the doorknob he turned and said, "There's a nice meeting room just off the lobby. I'm going to reserve it for ten o'clock in the morning. I'll have everybody there a few minutes early. I'll also bring you a bat plus a home plate. Anything else you need, Luther?"

"Nothing except their attention."

George nodded. "You'll have it, Luther."

2

True to his word, George Hauser had all the players seated in the meeting room when Luther Barber made his entrance. George stood before the group to say a few words. He looked tired and a little pale. The shadows were very deep around his eyes.

"Men, I've asked Luther to speak to you this morning about hitting, or in our case, why we are experiencing a lack of such hitting. The past few weeks has been a frustrating time for all of us. We cannot win in this league, or any league, with the kind of run production that we have been getting. We must start hitting, or the season will be a total loss. With this in mind I have asked Luther to talk with you this morning. I know you have marveled at the way he has handled opposing pitchers in this league. Since reporting for spring training in March, he has not had a single slump at the plate. He understands the mechanics of proper hitting, and this is why I am so pleased to have him before you this morning. He has nothing in his contract that states he must act as another coach on this club. He's here because he's confident that he can get us out of this mess. I know you will give him your undivided attention. If you have questions, field them before all of us.''

Turning toward the big first sacker, George said, ''Luther, these men are waiting to hear what you have to say.''

The strong man walked slowly to the front of the room. Picking up a long, slim-handled bat, he stared silently out over the group of Bears players. Then he started his talk.

''Manager Hauser assured me that all of you would show up this morning. I was sure you would not. I'll try not to waste your time. Hitting has always been easy for me. I've never experienced many slumps, but that doesn't mean that I know nothing about what causes hitting slumps. I've watched hundreds of hitters suffer through lean times at the plate. Slumps happen when the player leaves his natural way of swinging. He starts pressing and changes from good hitting habits to all the bad ones. In most cases he starts taking too many good hitting pitches. At the same time he starts swinging at too many pitches out of the strike zone. By taking too many pitches, he puts himself at the mercy of the pitcher. He's always trying to get a hit when he's behind in the count. In other words, he's forced to hit the pitcher's best pitch. In the long run, if you put yourself in that type of position, you're a loser as a successful hitter. I have noticed that we have several people on this club that have become this type of hitter. Middlecroft, you haven't swung at a first pitch strike in weeks! You're always hitting behind in the count. In spring training you were aggressive at the plate. You were jumping on some of those opening fastballs and driving the ball. What you have to do now is plain and simple. Cut down on your swing a little and drive the ball up the middle. When the curveball or fastball is to the outside of the plate, punch the ball in the hole to right field. Only try to pull the ball when the pitch is on the inside portion of the strike zone. Once you start making better contact, you can put a little more muscle in your swing. Miller, the same goes for you. For now try to hit those good strikes right back through the box. Both of you should follow the ball right down to the bat. If the ball is out of the strike zone, follow the ball right back into the catcher's mitt. This habit will keep you from taking your eyes off the ball on its flight to the plate. It will also improve your knowledge of the strike zone.''

Pausing for a few moments, Luther caught his breath and then continued. ''Reems, you're not making contact at all. You're moving your front shoulder out of the path of the pitch. You need to see more fastballs. All the pitchers of late have been curve-balling the socks off you. If I were managing this club, I would put you in the lead-off spot for a few games. Leading off you would see twice as many fastballs as you would down lower in the lineup. I have a feeling after you line a couple of those fastballs up the alley, you'll start getting back some of your confidence. I know you can hit a good curveball. I saw you straighten out a number of them in spring training. Right now you're too anxious, and you're chasing breaking balls off the outside corner. Take a few of those sucker pitches, and the pitchers will start bending the ball in the good hitting areas. I would suggest that you get up on the plate a little more to help you handle the curveball. You have fast hands, and I know you can handle that inside fastball.''

Luther then pointed a finger at the Bears second baseman. "Wilkins, you're a slap and punch hitter. Of late instead of slapping and punching, you're swinging hard enough to take both your feet off the ground. You also need to bunt more. In spring training you would drop one down the third base line. On your next trip, with the third baseman playing in close, you would pick on an outside pitch and punch the ball down into the left field corner. How many times have you tried that play in the past three weeks? I heard Hauser mention the same type of play to you better than two weeks ago. You tried it once and then went back to trying to pull the ball over the right field fence. With your speed you should be looking for the holes in the infield. Anytime you can move that third baseman in a step or two, you have a good chance of getting the ball by him. Once it's down the line and into the outfield, you can leg it into second base. Now, with a base hit we've got a run."

Looking around the room, Luther spotted outfielder Jack Goodman. "Goodman, come on up here."

The Bears centerfielder left his chair and walked to the front of the room.

Luther handed him a bat and asked him to take his present batting stance alongside the plate. When Goodman had settled himself in the batter's box, Luther had a question. "Is that the stance you used in spring training and during the first couple of weeks of the season?"

The outfielder shook his head. "I've always crowded the plate, but of late I've moved back a little because I was getting jammed with the fastball. They were sawing the bat off in my hands."

Luther took the bat and took a stance which placed him close to the plate. "There was nothing at all the matter with your old stance. I watched you in spring training, and you had one of the fastest pair of hands that I have ever seen. You were opening your hips in a hurry and getting the fat part of the bat on those inside fastballs. Two weeks into the season you got lazy with the bat. Instead of snapping it around, you were pulling it through the strike zone. When you changed your stance, you started having problems with the breaking pitches. Go back to your old stance and start using your hands the way you have in the past.''

Goodman smiled, and nodded in agreement.

Luther asked if anyone had a question. Barney Kerr's high voice sounded from the back of the room. ''Luther, you mentioned that we need to be more aggressive, that we need to jump on that first pitch. All of us have noticed that you almost always take the first pitch. How come?''

Without the slightest hesitation Luther made his reply. ''I have always considered myself a good one or two strike hitter. By looking at the first pitch, especially on my first trip to the plate against the pitcher, I get a good idea of his velocity if the pitch is a fastball. If it is a curveball, I get a good look at the sharpness of his breaking pitch. Most hitters cannot afford to put themselves in a hole by taking the first strike. I do not consider myself an average hitter. I do not need three strikes to hit the ball over the fence or up one of the alleys. I can do the job with one or two.''

There was some laughter around the room.

''I have only one more thing to say, and then I'm through. I don't believe that the pitching in this league is better than the hitters on this club. All pitchers would be tough if they could put the ball exactly where they desired in the strike zone. They cannot, and that's where we come in. When they make a mistake, we have to be aggressive and jump on the pitch. Maybe you'll only have one chance for each turn at bat. When you receive that chance, you have to make the most of the opportunity. Right now most of you are not making enough contact. Hit the ball some place, and sooner or later the hits will come. Tell yourself that you're better than the pitcher, and then prove it.''

Laying the bat aside, Luther murmured, ''That's

all I've got to say."

To a man, all the players were on their feet and gave the big man a loud ovation.

Luther Barber stood placidly before the group. His only sign of discomfort was the nervous trembling of his fingers that toyed with the buttons of his jacket. His face was no longer worn and guarded. Instead, a warm smile came forth, and for the moment his eyes brightened.

CHAPTER
11

TIME FOR HEROES

Ten days later — Connersburg.

Joel Travis knew he had to pay his young friend Dave a visit before catching the afternoon train up to Burlington. David Whittaker helped his Father farm a nice spread of rolling land just two miles east of the Travis property. The Whittakers still worked their place with top grade mules, and as Joel took a shortcut through a gentle sloping pasture field, he saw Dave plowing with three red sorrel mules. The beautiful animals, hooked up to a sulky plow, were probably 17 hands high, and their perspiring bodies glistened in the morning sun.

Dave Whittaker was a great strapping lad, broad and strong, and his face was as cheerful as the tune he whistled. When he noticed Joel, he shouted, "Fine plowing weather; come over to lend a hand?" The young farmer halted the mules and sat smiling on the weather beaten riding plow.

"Sorry, Dave," Joel answered, "I'm heading up to

Burlington this afternoon. By this evening I'll be pulling on a baseball uniform. I'll have to take a rain check on the plowing.''

Dave wrapped the reins around the seat of the plow and motioned toward a shady fence row at the end of the field. His eyes squinted under his straw hat. 'How's your ball club doing in that new league?''

Joel frowned a little. ''They got off to a bad start, losing twenty of the first thirty one games, but since then they've won eight of the last ten. They're starting to score some runs for the pitchers.''

David sat down beneath a small tree and tossed his hat upon a large stone. Wiping his brow with a red bandanna, the muscular youngster than flashed a wide grin. ''I suppose you're going up north and lead those fellas to another pennant.''

Joel laughed loudly. ''Listen, I'll be lucky if I can last seven or eight innings for awhile. Throwing down here is sure not like facing AA hitters in the Atlantic League.''

''How long before you'll be starting a ball game?''

Joel paused to find a sitting place on an old stone fence. ''I talked with George Hauser on the telephone yesterday. He said Joe Codrington had a stiff shoulder, and Welterroth had a nasty looking blood blister on the middle finger of his pitching hand. I'm starting against New London at their park tomorrow night.''

Dave's smile was bright. ''Nothing like going right from pasture to harness.''

Joel nodded. ''I'm a bit worried about my control, however. The secret of successful pitching is in staying ahead of the hitters. I know I can't get behind the type of hitters they have in that league. I've thrown a couple of pick up games down here of late, but the umpires have a much larger strike zone around Connersburg. My arm is well rested, and when I'm that strong, the ball is difficult to keep in the strike zone.''

The two young men remained silent for a number

of minutes. From over the fields came the breath of newly turned earth and the fragrance of wild flowers from the nearby woodlots. Joel studied the weathered face of his young friend. David's expression was one of calmness and serenity.

"You really love this place, don't you, Dave?"

The young man's eyes blurred a little. Joel knew the reaction did not come from the blazing sun.

"There's an awesome closeness about a farm like this one," replied Dave. "The land has such great strength. It casts a spell like a great cathedral. I guess I know every high and low spot on this entire place. By working the land with mules, Dad and I get a little closer to Nature and to the Man upstairs. I know a number of men who work the land like we do, Joey. They're good men, good with their hands and good with animals. There's something special about spending an entire day in the fields with hard working animals. When the day's work is over, when you lift the plow and start for the barn, when you feel the pull on the reins from the hungry mules, that's when the world seems right."

At length David reached into his back pocket to draw forth a wallet from which he abstracted a check. As he held the piece of paper before him, a pleasant smile crept across his face. "Joey, have you ever restored a piece of land?"

The question had caught Joel a little off guard. After a moment's hesitation he nodded soberly. "I guess all good farmers have restored a portion of land at one time or another. Father and I cleared that small field east of the Cliff Hutchinson place about five years ago. It was just weeds and stone, with the top soil about as hard as cement. We picked the stone, cut, hauled, and burned the weeds, and put dressing on the field. We put on an application of lime to sweeten the soil. The manure enriched the field chemically and added organic material to the soil. We got rid of all that dry, caked type of earth. Before long the top layer of the field was loose and open, with water being held instead of running off.

The field came back to life and started to produce some decent crops."

Dave smiled. "This check is for the ten acres across the road from the Blume place. Dad wrote the check this morning; I'll be taking it over to Tom Blume this evening. We're going to restore that chunk of land with some hard work and American know how. Tom's been under the weather for a good spell; you know that, Joey. He neglected the farm; he knows it, and he regrets it. Old Tom was pleased when Dad offered to buy the land and get started with the restoration. Can you think of anything more satisfying than turning a tired piece of earth into something full of life?"

"No, I really can't," answered Joel.

David placed the check back into his wallet. In a low, proud voice he announced, "Next week Dad and I are going over to Wallaceburg to look at more livestock. Good stock man by the name of Carl Joiner has a team of big mules for sale, blonde sorrels, 5 and 7 years old. If we can buy them right, Joey, we'll have them in our barn by the middle of next week. We'll need some more mule power around here with that extra acreage."

Joel had been listening avidly to his friends comments. Slowly he straightened from his sitting position atop the crumbled stone fence. His voice was soft and held a tone of admiration. "Looks as though you two have a very rewarding summer ahead. When I get back this coming fall, I'm going to come over and drive those new mules. You can show me what you've done to that new ten acres over at Tom Blume's place."

The two friends walked slowly back to the resting mules. Picking up the smooth reins, David said quietly, "You know, Joey, I can't express myself as well as you can, but I always figured that most people have a problem admitting their pleasure in simple and ordinary things. Every morning that I see the sun rising over that hill to the east, my heart beats a little faster. Whenever I work on our orchard, plant some new trees, or work the ground like today, I get the feeling that this is the original calling for me. I guess we all have a certain amount of natural talent to put to the best possible use. We're both fortunate to be able to have a place where we can work hard to enjoy and develop our talents. You're getting your chance at Burlington, and I'm receiving mine right here at home. Sort of lucky, aren't we, Joey?''

David paused for a moment to fumble with the worn reins. He then brought forth his right hand and clasped Joel's hand in a firm grip. ''Write, Joey, write and let me know how your pitching's coming. When I get your address, I'll keep you posted on what's going on back here in Connersburg. If I can be of any help over at your place this summer, just let me know. You brought a lot of joy and entertainment to all those folks up north last season. No reason why it should be any different this summer. I'll keep a close watch on your club in the papers.''

Joel stepped back as David clucked to the mules and the animals heaved into their harnesses. A few minutes later atop an adjoining hillside, Joel looked back at the partially furrowed field. He could see his young friend slumped slightly forward on the sulky riding plow. He could almost hear the happy notes of the boy's whistled tune.

2

Joel Travis was ready to start his first game of the season. As he made his way down to the bullpen to warm up, his heart was going a lot faster than his feet. He had not pitched in a single professional game since his appearance in the championship game last year. If he could last seven innings against this good hitting New London club, he would be more than pleased. George Hauser had asked him to go as far as he could.

Although the Bears league record was a weak 19-23, the hitters had recently started to sting the ball with some authority. The club was slowly pulling itself up through the standings with timely hitting,

good defense, and, up until the last few games strong
pitching. Burlington trailed fourth place New London
by only 3½ games.

The New London ball park was of new construc-
tion and therefore was experiencing some landscaping
problems. The playing area grass was not fully
developed, and the skin part of the infield was rough
and uneven in spots. The outfield fence distances
were very short, and on this evening the breeze was
blowing straight out from home plate.

In the bottom of the first inning Joel found
himself struggling with his control. He walked the
second and third men in the New London lineup, plus
he got behind in the count to the clean-up man.
When he came in with a low fastball, the hitter drove
a sharp ground ball through the Bears infield. The
base runner from second made the turn at third and
came across with the first run of the game. Joel got
the next hitter to pull a ground ball to Miller, and
the Bears third-sacker turned it into a fast double
play.

In the second and third innings Joel escaped
serious trouble, but in the fourth New London pushed
across another run. In the meantime, the Bears could
do little with a big right-hander on the mound for
New London. Burlington was down by two runs, and

the home town hurler was pitching as if the 2-0 lead would be more than enough to put the game in the "Blue Sox" win column.

Joel gave up three more walks in the fifth and sixth innings, but a nice running catch by Jack Goodman in the fifth, and another quick double play by the infield in the sixth, kept New London off the scoreboard. In the bottom of the seventh, however, the big New London catcher caught hold of a high fastball and drove it well over the 375 mark in left center. When Joel left the game for a pinch-hitter in the top of the eighth, Burlington was down 3-0. At the end of the game the same 3-0 score prevailed.

In the clubhouse George Hauser made it a point to visit Joel in front of his locker. The manager was disappointed in being shut out, but he seemed pleased with his young right-hander's pitching. "Not bad; not bad at all for a first outing, Joey. You were throwing hard in those late innings, still challenging the hitters. Control was shaky, but we expected that, didn't we?"

Joel nodded in total agreement. "I was up and down and all over the place. I was lucky to last seven innings with all those 3 and 1, and 3 and 2 counts. I just couldn't stay in front with my fastball. It was sailing high most of the night."

George gave his pitcher a friendly slap on the back. "You're going to be just fine. Don't worry about your loss tonight. As it worked out, it was an ideal time to get some work in. We caught that right-hander for New London at the wrong time."

After showering and dressing, Joel joined the other players on the team bus. After a short ride downtown, the players either entered the hotel or found themselves a restaurant close to their lodging. Joel and Ken Lambert found a small eating place within walking distance.

After ordering, the two players relaxed and discussed the night's ball game. At a table directly behind the players sat four men. Two of the middle aged customers wore dark blue New London baseball caps. As Joel was about to say something to Lambert, one of the men turned his chair toward the players and in a beligerent tone of voice asked, "Are you guys members of that rag tag ball club from Burlington?"

Ken Lambert motioned to Joel to ignore the remark. It was apparent the man had been drinking something more than coffee.

When the man received no answer from the players, another man at the table shouted, "What's the matter? Something wrong with you guy's hearing? My friend here asked you a question. Are you bums with that outfit from Burlington?"

In the dimly lit restaurant Joel could only see half of the eating area, but it was obvious that only a couple of young waitresses had been left behind to close up the establishment.

The four husky men were becoming more warlike by the minute. The next comment was meant for Joel. "Doesn't surprise me they can't hear," growled one of the men. "They've got all kinds of misfits on that club. They even had a crippled kid trying to pitch tonight. Wonder what they'll wheel out there tomorrow night!"

Ken Lambert and Joel pushed their chairs back. Four good sized men against a youngster and a small outfielder was not the best of odds, but the players were taking no more from the occupants of the nearby table. The four men were on their feet, moving menacingly toward the ball players. Suddenly a calm voice sounded directly behind Joel.

"Getting so a couple of gentlemen have trouble enjoying a quiet meal and a little conversation. Always seems there's a few loud mouths around to spoil the occasion."

Luther Barber was dressed in a tight blue shirt and a pair of thin slacks. His bulging muscles seemed to ripple beneath the summer clothing. Picking up a steel framed chair, he used both his massive hands to bend the metal completely out of its original shape. The four men were having second thoughts about the altercation.

Luther walked slowly around the players' table. With a cat like move, he grabbed one of the men and twisted his arm up sharply behind his back. There was a loud cry of pain. The other three men did not move.

Luther had his left arm around the man's neck. "Now you're going to apologize to this young man for that misfit, cripple remark. Then you're going to apologize to both of these players for interrupting their meal!"

When Luther gave a quick jerk on the man's arm, the two apologies streamed from the man's mouth. Luther then released the man and pushed him toward his friends.

The burly infielder's voice steadied, "Pay your bill and get out!"

The four men mumbled beneath their breaths, but they wasted no time paying their checks and leaving the restaurant.

Both players thanked the big first baseman for getting them out of a dangerous situation. They asked him to join them at the table, but he declined, saying he had lost his appetite. Before leaving, he turned to the young pitcher and said, "Sort of livened up a dull evening, didn't it!"

CHAPTER 12

MOMENTUM

Luther Barber settled his own score with New London. In the second game of the three game set he drove in four runs with two towering home runs. The

Bears came away with a 6-2 win behind the six hit pitching of Tom Wyant. In the final game, the hard hitting infielder cleared the bases with a ringing double and then poked a home run that decided the contest in the ninth inning. Carl Zoltowski picked up the win with two perfect innings of relief work.

When the club moved to Pottstown, a club only 2 games out of first place, the Bears were eager to put on their uniforms. Most of the hitters were now making good contact, and the defense had not committed an error in three ball games. Pete Gleason got the call for the opening game of the series.

Frank Knight had been working hard with the little southpaw from Hanover. He smoothed out the left-handers motion by making the pitcher pass through his complete motion without the slightest hesitation. He gave the young hurler another pitch by teaching him a screwball. Gleason had been having some trouble with right-hand hitters, hitters with quick bats. These hitters were jumping on Gleason's fastball with regularity. Frank gave the Bears lefty a little screwball that fell away from the right hand hitters. With the change of speed on the pitch it gave the hitter something else to think about. It made Gleason's fastball a great deal more effective.

For seven innings against Pottstown, Pete Gleason was near perfect. The only thing he had given up was a two out walk in the third inning. The Burlington hitters, on the other hand, were having a field day with Pottstown pitching. Chet Miller had mashed two doubles, driving in four runs. Hal Meadowcroft had a two run homer to go with a run producing double. Luther Barber had hit his 14th round tripper.

There were no secrets as to what was going on. Gleason had a no-hitter with only six more outs to record. The defensive players were feeling the pressure right along with the little lefty. George Hauser made two changes in his lineup before the Bears took the field in the eighth. Ken Lambert, a top defensive player, was inserted in left field, and

Carruthers replaced Luther at first base.

The first hitter for Pottstown in the bottom of the eighth hit a shot directly at Chet Miller. The Bears third sacker knocked the drive down and threw the runner out by half a step. Gleason worked hard on the next hitter, but lost him on a 3-2 count. Taking his time with the next hitter, the southpaw finally came down with a good breaking ball which the batter hit sharply in the hole to the right of Kerr. The little shortstop grabbed the ball and fired to Wilkins who in turn gunned the ball to Carruthers. The inning was over.

In the top of the ninth the Bears went down in order. Gleason walked quickly to the mound for the last half of the inning.

The first man up for Pottstown was a little shortstop with good running speed. George Hauser waved Chet Miller in a couple of steps from his normal third base position. The fleet-footed Pottstown infielder tried to push a bunt past the mound, but Gleason pounced on the roller and threw the runner out in plenty of time. When the left-hander returned to the mound, a wave of encouragement rolled in from the Bears' defensive unit. The entire Burlington non-playing roster were up on the top step of the dugout.

The next hitter for Pottstown ran the count to 2-2, then hit a low flyball down the right field line. When it left the bat, it looked as though it might drop in fair territory, but at the last moment it seemed to bear right and landed only a few inches in foul ground. On the next delivery the hitter lofted an easy flyball to Goodman in center field.

The Pottstown manager sent up a slim right-hand hitter to pinch-hit for his regular second baseman. Once in the box the batter choked up several inches on his bat to make some type of contact.

Pete Gleason took a few deep breaths and looked down for his sign. Still nice and smooth in the wind-up, the pitcher brought a good fastball toward the plate. The batter punched at the pitch and hit a short line drive into short left center. Ken Lambert in left field was just too far away to reach the ball. The only man for Burlington with a chance to reach the short flyball was Jack Goodman in center field. Barney Kerr, with his back to the infield, watched helplessly as the ball passed over his head. Goodman, running at top speed, closed fast on the falling baseball. Just before he reached the crucial area, Goodman folded one leg beneath his hips and slid across the damp outfield grass. He made the catch in a sitting position with the glove in his lap. Within seconds he was up on his feet and showing the ball to the umpire. In the dugout the Burlington players raced to the mound to congratulate Pete Gleason. From there they hurried to meet Jack Goodman. After the veteran fly chaser had presented Gleason with the baseball, he was lifted to the shoulders of several teammates. Luther Barber and Stuart Reems had Gleason on their shoulders, and the two were giving the Burlington left-hander a free ride around the infield.

In the clubhouse Gleason grabbed Goodman in a big bear hug. His words echoed the sentiments of the entire Burlington ball club. "Jack, I'm sure I'll get most of the newspaper print, but you deserve half of it. When I saw the ball pass over the infield, I just about gave up hope. Then I saw you coming at full steam, and I thought maybe, just maybe, you might have a chance. I've never witnessed such a catch before, and I'll have to live a mighty long time to see that one tonight duplicated."

George Hauser entered the conversation. "Pete, those kinds of catches just don't happen. I've watched Jack practice that type of catch for the past two years. When you do your home work, you pass the test!"

Gleason nodded in agreement and added, "You're so right, Skip."

2

The no-hitter seemed to stoke up the furnace in the Burlington Express engine room. The momentum

of the ball club was like a fast passenger train
heading downhill and running a few minutes behind
schedule. At Tyler City the Bears took three out of
four and took over fourth place. In the next two
weeks the Burlington ball club stunned their
competitors by winning 11 of 13 games, and by
winning them with some of the best baseball ever
played in the Atlantic League. Joel, supported by
some lusty hitting, ran off three wins in a row. Tom
Wyant and Pete Gleason put two games apiece in the
win column, and Doty, along with Zoltowski, came
out of the bullpen to pitch inspiring baseball. Joe
Codrington and Welterroth were back in rotation,
and each had notched a victory in the past week.

As for the hitting, it was difficult to name a
leader. It seemed a new hero was born for each game
on the weekly schedule. Hal Meadowcroft had been
on a tear with 15 runs batted in over the last 14
games. Chet Miller had his batting average up to
321, and Jack Goodman was leading the league in
doubles. Barney Kerr and Stuart Reems had started
several rallies with key hits, and both were closing in
on the 300 mark. McCoy and Wilkins were still
struggling a little, but both were showing signs of
getting back into a solid groove. As for Luther
Barber, the power man was not letting up a bit on
Atlantic League opposing pitchers. His 21 home runs
led the league as did his 64 runs batted in. The first
baseman's 296 batting average was the third best on
the club.

The Bears were presently sitting in third place,
but the first four clubs in the standings were tightly
bunched.

BAINBRIDGE	42-26
POTTSTOWN	40-28
BURLINGTON	37-31
TEAL CITY	36-32

Back home the Bears kept the pressure on
Bainbridge and Pottstown by taking three out of four
from Wheelersburg. Joel notched his 10th victory
with a fine four hitter. Frank Knight had shown him

a better grip for his curveball. He now placed his index and middle fingers to the left of the seams (where they are the narrowest on the baseball). This enabled him to pull down on the seams and give the curveball much more down spin. Frank had told him to always return the baseball to the plate umpire when he noticed a baseball with flat seams. As the veteran pitching coach explained, "The seams are placed on the baseball for two reasons. First, to keep the cover together. Secondly, to benefit the pitcher. Any smart pitcher should study the position of the seams on the ball and use them to his full advantage."

Frank Knight also kept telling the young pitcher about, throwing through the catcher's target, not just at it. The elderly coach explained it this way. "Joey, sometimes if you just throw at the catcher's glove you have a tendency to aim the ball. In other words you throw the baseball like you would throw a dart at a dartboard. Now if you try to throw the baseball through the catcher's target, you're going to throw unrestrained, hard, and fluid. It's like running to first base. If you just concentrate on running to the bag, you more than likely will let up a little just before you reach the bag. But, on the other hand, if you concentrate on running through the bag, or let's say 15 feet beyond, you most certainly will hit the base at full speed. Understand?" Joel understood. Frank Knight had a special way of explaining his theories. As a theorist in baseball, Joel felt the man had no equal.

Into July the first four clubs set a torrid pace. By August Burlington was 16 games over 500 in the standings, but they were having problems staying in third place. Teal City had a fighting bunch of ball players who kept coming back to win games in the late innings. Bainbridge was hanging tough, just winning enough games to stay on top. In the second division Wheelersburg kept creeping up, just waiting for one of the first division clubs to hit a losing streak. Wheelersburg had a number of older players who knew all about a stretch run to the playoffs.

Through August Luther Barber proved the difference between retaining third place and slipping back into the second division. His booming home runs turned a number of games around and put them in the Burlington win column. At a time when most power hitters in the league were getting tired and having trouble getting the ball out of the ball parks, Luther's great strength seemed not to ebb the slightest. On September first at LaSalle the burly first baseman hit his 38th and 39th round trippers. The following evening he drove a fastball over the center field fence to reach the 40 mark. His 126 runs batted in total easily led the league.

Luther had his own explanation for late season power success. ''I always go to a little lighter bat in the month of August. I also try to pull the ball a little more. I wait on a pitch that I can smack out in front of the plate. When the season starts to wind down, you're naturally a little tired. By pulling more, I shoot for the shortest part of the ball park, right down the line. Those long home runs into right center are fine for me during the early part or mid-part of the season, but as the season enters the final portion I take that outside pitch and wait for something with which I can pull the trigger a little quicker. Something else I try to remember. Late in the season I get a lot of off-speed pitches, so I concentrate on keeping my bat back in the set position. I may shift a little weight to my front foot, but I always try to keep the bat uncommitted. Any power hitter must do this to generate home-run power. In late season I get very few fastballs to hit, so I work on hitting the breaking pitches. If I have to swing at a curveball on the outside portion of the plate, I try to rake or sweep the ball into the left field stands. I'm strong enough to do that type of thing.''

During the first week of September Luther pulled a game out of the loss column by a bit of sound, smart power hitting. With the score 4-3 and Burlington on the short end, Luther came up to the

plate with one out and Chet Miller on first base. The Pottstown right-hander threw the big man a straight change which seemed to be in good location, low at the knees and away. Luther had shifted some of his weight to his front foot, but his bat was back in the starting position. The black piece of wood came around in a sweeping swing which pulled the ball directly down the left field line. The high fly ball just cleared the fence at the foul pole. In a way the home run was a bit cheap, but in the box score it looked like a tape measure shot.

In the north woods of our timber country there's an old saying that, somehow or other, the really talented woodchopper, one whose chips always fly away from him and never into his eyes, whose whistling chops always cut square and fairly into the wood and never glance, has a way of helping his ax perform by shouting, "Hep!" as the blade hits the target. Luther Barber would have made some kind of a lumberjack. His bat seemed to always hit the ball squarely. He also had a habit of grunting, "Hep!" when he knew the ball was ticketed for home run territory.

CHAPTER

13

BAD START

During the last week of the season Teal City put on a rush and took over second place. Pottstown hit the skids and dropped to fourth place. Burlington played steady baseball and held on to third place. Bainbridge won the pennant by two full games.

The post season playoffs would have the first place finisher playing the third place club in a best four-out-of-seven series. At the same time the second place ball club would be playing the fourth place team in the same type of setup. Burlington would be playing the first two games of their series at Bainbridge. The next three were scheduled at Burlington, and, if needed, the last two would be played back at Bainbridge.

George Hauser named Joel to start the series. He would be opposed by Sheldon Lindley, Bainbridge's outstanding left-hand pitcher.

Joel felt good warming up in the bullpen deep down into the right field corner of the spacious Bainbridge stadium. Ed Wickland took his warmup pitches without comment. However, when he had finished and grabbed his jacket, the veteran catcher said quietly, "You're going to have good stuff tonight, Joey. Just make sure you keep your pitches in the right location."

Through the first four innings neither pitcher faltered the slightest. In the fifth Bainbridge put together a double and single to record the first run of the game. Lindley was showing why he was considered the finest southpaw in the Atlantic League. Through the seventh inning he had given up

only two hits, and Hal Meadowcroft had both of them. Going into the eighth Bainbridge held doggedly to their one run lead.

Joel got into a little trouble in the eighth when he walked the leadoff hitter, and the next batter bunted him along to second. The next hitter lined a pitch cleanly into right field. McCoy took the ball on one hop and unleashed a low, fast moving throw toward the plate. Meadowcroft threw his mask aside and awaited the throw. The base runner coming down from third tried to slide around the big catcher's tag, but Meadowcroft took the throw belt high and applied the big catcher's mitt containing the ball to the sliding runner's left leg. The plate umpire gave the overhand motion with his arm and shouted, "You're out!"

Joel was behind the plate in line with the throw when it came in from the arm of McCoy. The ball never tailed, nor did it die when it hit the grass in the infield. McCoy delivered the throw overhand, not three quarter or side arm, and he followed through with his body after letting the ball go. It was a 250 foot strike from right field.

McCoy had been making this kind of throw ever since Joel joined the club nearly two years ago. The quiet outfielder had cut down more than a few baserunners with his powerful and accurate arm. Stuart Reems in left did his part for the club with his big bat. Jack Goodman in center and McCoy in right saved the Bears pitchers countless runs with their great glove and arm work.

In the top of the ninth Burlington threatened but did not score. Joel had given up but four hits and one run while striking out 13. Lindley had been even better. The left-hander had allowed but three singles while setting down 14 Burlington batters on strikes. The game had been played in less than two hours.

George Hauser had nothing but praise for his club's performance. "Joey pitched a truly great game. The defense played the way that they're capable of playing. Unfortunately we ran into a mighty fine pitcher this evening. It's been a good long time since any hurler handed our hitters in that fashion. Tonight was his night. Next time I'm betting we'll get to him."

The following night Pete Gleason was named to even up the series. Gleason spoke quite impersonally, with a quiet assurance that was more impressive than loud assertions. "I'm ready to pitch a good ball game. If we can score a few runs, we can go back home with a split."

Bainbridge started a stocky right-hander by the name of Sid Barnhart. In the top of the first, with one out, he walked the bases full. Stuart Reems got one run in with a long fly ball, but Meadowcroft grounded into a fast double play to end the inning. Gleason retired Bainbridge in order in the bottom half.

Through the fourth inning, Gleason kept Bainbridge at bay. In the fifth he had some control problems and two walks led to a run. The game remained tied going into the seventh inning.

Leading off, Eddie Wilkins punched a single between short and third. Kerr moved him down to second. Chet Miller popped up to the Bainbridge second baseman. Luther Barber came to the plate. Bainbridge wanted no part of the big slugger and gave him a free pass. With Stuart Reems at the plate the Bainbridge manager made a pitching change. He brought in a big awkward looking reliefer by the name of Patterson.

At second, Eddie Wilkins took a sizable lead. It was at this point that the relief pitcher made the defensive play of the game. Stepping on the rubber, he then took his sign from his catcher. After pausing in his stretch, he suddenly whirled and with a quick movement fired the ball knee high over the second base bag. The move caught little Eddie by surprise. He tried frantically to get back to the base in time, but the Bainbridge second baseman applied a quick tag. The umpire gave the out sign, and the Burlington rally was over.

Chet Miller brought the infielder's glove out to

him. Wilkins was furious with himself. "How in the world can you get caught off a base when you're in scoring position with the go ahead run? How can a ball player be so thick headed? Geeze, Hauser must be pulling out what little hair he has left!"

Miller tried to calm the second baseman down. "Forget it, Eddie. The guy made a great move off the mound and the play was timed to perfection. Forget it! As far as this game's concerned we're still even with them."

In the bottom half of the seventh Bainbridge scored again when Stevens, a good hitting catcher, drove one of Gleason's curveballs over the 375 mark in left center.

In the top of the eighth Kenny Lambert tied the game with a run producing single up the middle. For the bottom half of the inning manager George Hauser sent in Carl Zoltowski to face a medley of right-hand hitters.

The Burlington relief specialist got into hot water when he walked the leadoff man. When the next hitter successfully moved the base runner along, George Hauser put the next hitter on. The Bears needed a double play ball in the worst way.

After running up a full count, Zoltowski got the next hitter to ground a breaking ball into the hole between short and third. The ball was not hit sharply and took three high hops before it reached Barney Kerr's glove. The shortstop grabbed the ball and fired to Wilkins at second. Eddie, realizing that he had no play at first, came across the bag and gunned the ball to Chet Miller at third. The Bainbridge runner had rounded the bag. Scrambling back, the baserunner tried to grab the base with his right hand. Miller brought the ball down quickly. The third base umpire gave the safe sign. The Bears third baseman was furious. George Hauser was out of the dugout in an instant and was following the base umpire down the left field line, arguing every step of the way. His voice could be heard back into the Bears' dugout.

"You missed it! You missed it, and you were

standing out of position! That man was tagged twice
before he reached the bag! How in the world can you
miss a play like that!"

The umpire stopped walking, folded his arms
across his chest, and gazed off into space. George kept
shouting into the umpire's face. The noses of the two
baseball men were nearly touching. As Joel watched
from the dugout, the umpire suddenly stepped aside,
brought up his right arm in a sweeping motion, and
threw the manager out of the game. Apparently
George had used a few words that were not in his
usually fine vocabulary. Before leaving, the Bears'
manager got his money's worth. Joel was sure the
umpire's ears were hot enough to light a few
matches.

In the dugout George stopped for a minute to talk
with Frank Knight. "Take over, Frank. Stick with
Zoltowski. It's his game to win or lose." The
Burlington manager then walked from the dugout

and made his way around to the visitors' clubhouse.

Joel was sure that Hauser heard what happened next. Zoltowski fired a fastball, and the batter promptly lashed it into left field for a clean single. Bainbridge had a 3-2 lead.

In the ninth Patterson shut the Bears off without a baserunner. Burlington would be returning home, down two games in the first playoff series.

In the clubhouse, George Hauser made the rounds consoling his ball players. Most of the players sat quietly in front of their small quarters where their street clothes hung on simple wall hangers. Most had their heads bowed, or were slowly removing their sweat-soaked uniforms.

When all the players had showered and dressed, George called a brief meeting. The tone of his voice was light. In his eyes was a warm, timidly ingratiating grope for good will. "We're not out of this thing, boys; don't think that for a minute. We're going back home, and the bats are going to pick us up. Our pitching has been good enough to win. I've got a feeling it's going to be just as good from here on in. They still have to whip us two more times, and I don't believe they can do it. We have Tom Wyant here ready to go on Saturday. Welterroth's ready to go on Sunday. Joey can come back on Monday. Tomorrow we'll take advantage of the off day and hold a workout at the stadium. Everybody be out at the park a little before nine thirty. We'll call it a day by noon."

After stopping for something to eat, the bus headed back to Burlington. Joel sat with Luther Barber. The brawny slugger felt confident about the playoff picture. "I think George Hauser's right about the next few games. Lindley's a good left-hander, but he's never going to throw another game against us like that one the other night. Wyant, Welterroth, and yourself are very capable of really shutting off their hitters. When you get past Lindley, the rest of their staff is very mediocre. Stop their hitting, score a few runs, and we can win this series."

110

Joel felt he had to ask a question. "Aren't you selling a first place club a little short?"

Luther shook his head. "They finished in first place, but they were struggling the last few weeks. The best club in the stretch was Teal City. I look for them to polish off Pottstown. I have the feeling we're going to lock horns with those boys from Teal City."

Joel went back over Luther's remarks. He felt uncertainty, nervousness, as if Luther had miscalculated some place. Yet there was this great feeling of confidence in the man's voice.

Before Joel leaned his head back to catch a few winks, Luther made one more comment. "Remember one more thing about these playoffs, Joey. This is a veteran ball club. It's also a great defensive ball club. Most ball players are easily upset under pressure. The best advice is to stay cool and let the opponent beat himself!"

Joel knew Luther took his professional baseball very seriously. That was the only way to take it. Once during another bus ride the big man had said, "Professional golf is a serious battle — not a hiking expedition. Even in professional bridge playing, it's a clash of wits — not a gathering for an evening of gossip. Whenever you play a professional sport, you play to win. You play hard, and you play square. If you always play with that attitude, you can accept defeat."

CHAPTER

14

OLIVIA

Before the workout Friday morning, Joel stopped by Luther's locker. The veteran was applying shoe polish to a nearly new pair of baseball spikes. When he had finished the application he quickly brushed the shoes and hung them by the laces on a nail at the back of his locker. Noticing Joel's interest, he remarked, "That's an old habit of mine. Years ago, just before an important series, I just happen to hang a pair of spikes up in that same fashion. Well, for the next few days I hit baseballs like I had never hit them before. We won the East Texas League championship and I've been hanging spikes from the wall ever since. I figured I'd get the job done this morning. You know, just before Bainbridge comes to town."

George Hauser limited the workout to a brief batting practice session and some running for the pitchers. Joel had just finished his last lap across the outfield when he heard his name called. Owner Harley Walsh was walking slowly toward him.

"Joel, can you spare me a few minutes?"

"Yes, sir," replied the young pitcher.

Harley's eyes squinted under his straw hat. "Joel, I received a telephone call this morning from a Mrs. Arthur Tillinghast. The Tillinghasts live over on the south side of town and have an eleven year old daughter by the name of Olivia. The girl is an avid baseball fan and follows our ball club on the radio. I say radio, because this past spring she was hit by an automobile in front of the Tillinghast's home; Olivia has been bedridden since the accident occurred on the

18th of April. She came home from the hospital last month, but I'm afraid she's not been doing very well. Mrs. Tillinghast mentioned that the doctors feel that she will recover; however, it's going to be a long process. The danger lies in her present attitude; she doesn't really believe what the medical people have been saying. The healing has been such a slow process that it's hardly noticeable to Olivia. She's a very discouraged young lady."

Harley paused for a few moments before continuing. "Mrs. Tillinghast was wondering if perhaps it might be possible to have two or three of our players pay Olivia a visit. When she mentioned her idea to her daughter, the girl asked about yourself, Joe Codrington, and Luther Barber. I've already talked to Joe and Luther. Both can visit the girl this afternoon at three o'clock. Can you make it?"

"Yes, sir, I'll be there." replied Joel. "I'll have my lunch in town, and head over that way a few minutes before three. I'll take a couple of auto-graphed baseballs with me."

Harley smiled, "I knew I could count on you, Joey."

In mid-afternoon Joel found himself walking down a tree-shaded street on Burlington's south side. He found 618 to be a small, squarish house with a slanting roof and a squat center chimney. At the walk leading up to the front steps stood a white, latched, wooden gate. Joel entered the yard and made his way to the front door. Before he could ring the bell, the door opened and a lovely lady stood before him. The woman was wearing a soft, gray silk dress and a dainty little Swiss apron with satin bows on the pockets. Her smooth black hair was entirely untouched with gray and lay soft, wavy, and abundant over her temples. There was hardly any suggestion of a wrinkle in her placid and kindly face.

"I'll bet you're Joel," she noted cheerfully. "Please come in. Mr. Codrington and Mr. Barber are waiting for you in the living room."

In the comfortable sitting room Mrs. Tillinghast

offered a quiet apology. "You gentlemen caught me working in the kitchen. I thought perhaps you might enjoy some tea and a cookie while visiting with Olivia." After a moment's pause she added, "If you would like to follow me, I'll show you to our daughter's room."

Mrs. Tillinghast led the way down a narrow hallway. What struck every one of the players was the unearthly quiet. Joel had never been in such a ghastly stillness in all his life.

Within seconds they were led into a small pink bedroom with the atmosphere charged with the fragrance of flowers. In a tiny bed was a small, slender girl, very pale, with shy blue eyes. Two puffy pillows elevated her head slightly from the surface of the bed. Her thin little face sharpened into a faint smile when the players entered the room.

Three chairs were positioned around the girl's bed. The players seated themselves, and Mrs. Tillinghast announced warmly, "Olivia, I would like to introduce pitcher Joel Travis, pitcher Joe Codrington, and first baseman Luther Barber." After a brief pause she noted, "Now if you people will excuse me for a few minutes, I will return to my kitchen. I am sure the four of you will find a great many interesting things to talk about." Turning quickly on her heel, the girl's mother exited the room.

Few human hearts have beaten out even the measure of five and fifteen years without feeling the deep love of a child. Almost every Christian, man or woman, has at heart the wish to heal the hurts of life for others, but few have the delicate tact which can touch a wound without giving pain. For the next thirty minutes the players visited with ailing Olivia Tillinghast, finding at times that the emotion within the room was nearly too much to endure. Efforts to cheer the girl proved to be futile. When the youngster spoke of her painful condition, tears rained down her cheeks. It was at this point that Luther Barber moved his chair a bit closer to the girl's bed and held her hand in both of his own. In a soft voice he said,

"Olivia, you are going to get much better in the weeks ahead. You must believe me. You must have faith. Your Mother told me that you say your prayers every single night. I say mine too, and I try to pray with my heart, just as a child like yourself would do. It does not matter so much about what words you use, but it matters very much whether you pray with your heart or with your lips. So many nice things can happen if we have faith and use all our strength. Do you believe me, Olivia?"

Through tears the frail girl answered, "I want to, but I can't find enough strength to fight how bad I feel. The hurt is too big for me to do anything about it. It's impossible."

"What's impossible, Olivia?"

"For me to get better. Some things are impossible, no matter how hard we try."

For several minutes the only sound in the room was the gentle sobbing of the little girl. Joel had never felt so helpless in his entire life. Joe Codrington sat with bowed head, his hands clasped tightly before him. Luther rose from his chair and left the room. He was gone for a number of minutes, and when he returned he was accompanied by Mrs. Tillinghast. Again drawing up his chair near the bed, Luther spoke to the girl in a soothing voice. "Olivia, I know you're a very loyal Burlington fan. I also know you understand baseball very well. Now, what would you say might be the hardest thing for any hitter to do at home plate?"

Olivia closed her eyes for a moment, and then reopening them, answered, "I would say hitting a home run."

Luther nodded, "I agree with you completely. Now would you say it's possible to hit a home run just because you feel like it?"

Olivia shook her head slightly. "No," was the brief answer.

Luther leaned a little closer to the girl. "Do you believe if I tried with all my strength, tried with every ounce of strength in my entire body, and asked for additional strength from the Lord in my little prayer tonight, do you think I could hit a home run especially for you in tomorrow's game? Do you believe that I could actually do that?''

Olivia turned her head ever so slightly and studied the big infielder's face. The girl's eyes brightened, and her voice seemed a little stronger when she answered. "You could do that by trying with all your strength and asking for help in your prayer, Luther?''

''I could do it,'' answered the big man. ''I could do it if you give me all your help, Olivia. Tomorrow you say to yourself, 'Luther's going to hit that home run. Nothing in this world's impossible, and somehow Luther's going to drive that baseball over the fence.' And you know something else? You're going to hit a home run for me. Oh, not tomorrow, but in the weeks ahead you're going to start feeling better, and before you can say Burlington Bears Baseball, you're going to be up and around, and doing all the things you used to do. Is that a deal, young lady? Can we shake hands on it?''

Olivia raised her right hand from the top of the covers, and Luther enclosed it with his two massive hands. Mrs. Tillinghast brushed a tear from her eye with the lower part of her apron. Joel felt a tight knot developing in his throat, and his eyes were so misty that he could barely make out the figures in the room.

Mrs. Tillinghast poured out the tea and carried the first cup to Luther. She served the other players, asking if anyone wished to use the sugar tongs or the little silver pitcher of cream.

At exactly four o'clock, the players said their goodbyes to the Tillinghasts. Beyond the wooden front gate Joe Codrington heaped his anger upon Luther Barber. His words were biting, and the pitcher's face was contorted into an ugly mask. ''Barber, that was the biggest grandstand play I've ever heard of! Do you realize what you've done? Can you imagine the feelings of that little girl when you fail to produce tomorrow? You're crazy to risk that girl's life to beef up your own ego!'' After walking away, the veteran pitcher turned and shouted, ''I thought I was beginning to understand you, Barber. What a waste of time!''

Luther paid no attention to the pitcher's remarks. He merely pulled his straw hat down tight around his ears and started walking up the street.

Joel shouted, ''Luther, wait! Please wait!'' He caught up with the older man in the middle of the block.

Joel pleaded with his teammate. ''Don't be mad at Joe, Luther. He's sort of mixed up in his thinking. He's just plain worried about Olivia, just like we are. He never meant all those things he said back there.''

Luther only grunted, and kept right on walking. When the two players reached Jefferson Avenue, separation point for Joel, the late afternoon sun was starting to slant its glimmering rays through the crowns of the tall oaks. Luther paused to put his arm across the young pitcher's shoulders. For a long moment he said not a word. When he did speak his voice was sympathetic and assuring.

''Don't concern yourself with the job I have to do tomorrow, Joey. Codrington can think what he wants about me; I've got more important things on my mind. I know what my odds are tomorrow, and they're not as bad as you might think. One more thing, young man, I'm going to call Codrington when I get back to my place. Only five people know about what has to be done tomorrow, and it's important that we keep it that way. Keep all that talk this afternoon under your hat.''

With a wave of his hand, the Burlington strong man shuffled off into the late afternoon shadows.

2

Joel Travis, awakening slowly, cocked his half opened eyes at the white-chintzed window in his room. The sound of driving rain against the glass, caused his body to stiffen. Tossing aside a light sheet on his bed, he hurried to the window. Outside the low dark clouds hung over the city like early morning mist in a swampish bog. Joel dressed in a hurry and walked quickly to a small restaurant near his apartment. After breakfast he caught a cab out to the ball park.

The third game of the Burlington-Bainbridge series was scheduled for one thirty P.M. The first person Joel noticed at the stadium was groundskeeper Ernie Groves.

"What's the forecast, Mr. Groves?"

"Not as bad as you might think, Joey. It's suppose to stop raining within the hour. We're not going to get any sunshine, but if the rain stops we can make the field playable."

Joel decided to stick around the park and wait for the rest of the players.

Neither club took batting practice due to the condition of the infield. Puddles of water were scattered about in the outfield, but as Ernie Groves had promised, the field was in playable condition. The crowd seemed undaunted by the miserable atmospheric situation. By one o'clock there was not a single vacant seat in the stadium.

To Joel it seemed everything was starting to stack up against Luther Barber. Shortly before game time a strong cold wind started blowing in from straight away center field. He had heard Chet Miller say, "You can forget about anyone hitting a ball out of this place today." The remark had sent a sudden chill throughout Joey's entire body. With no batting practice the hitters would have a tough time getting loose at the plate. Joey was more than a little worried.

Tom Wyant took the hill for the Bears, and the umpire behind the plate yelled, "Play Ball!"

The crafty right-hander for the home club had little trouble with Bainbridge in the top of the first inning. One ground ball had looked like a base hit, but the runner had trouble covering ground in the soggy base path. Barney Kerr put a little extra on his throw and retired the hitter by half a step.

118

Under normal circumstances Luther Barber usually sat down at the far end of the bench until he moved to the batters-up circle. However, Joel noticed that this afternoon he was sitting on the top step of the dugout studying Eldon Usher, the Bainbridge pitcher. Joey could not help but notice the strain on the big first baseman's rugged face. He looked tired, as if sleep had eluded him completely.

Luther got his chance to bat in the bottom of the first frame when Chet Miller blooped a single into short left field. Joey moved down to the steps of the dugout. His stomach ached from the tension.

Luther took more time than usual before he stepped into the batter's box. Once in, he took his usual stance with the big black bat pointed straight up from his hands.

Usher took his stretch and fired a good moving fastball toward the plate. Luther swung hard and fouled the pitch out of play. Usher rubbed up a new baseball and looked down for another sign. The next pitch was a curveball that picked up the outside corner for a called strike. Luther had seemed uninterested in the delivery.

After wasting a pitch, Usher brought forth another fastball up in the letters. Luther took a hard swing and the ball shot off the bat and headed for deep left center field. Joey jumped to his feet as the ball soared toward the 380 mark. The centerfielder for Bainbridge raced to the fence and then moved in several steps to catch the ball in front of the warning track. Joel's shoulders slumped. The ball had been hit hard, but the wind had brought the drive back into the ball park. Luther waited in the middle of the diamond for someone to bring him out his big first baseman's mitt.

Tom Wyant was working hard to keep the visitors off the scoreboard. In the second and third innings the seasoned pitcher set down six hitters in a row. Wyant was a money pitcher who always seemed to pitch his best baseball when the chips were down. With the Bears down by two games in the playoff series, Wyant was putting everything he had into each pitch. Conditions on the mound were causing problems for both pitchers. Wyant had nearly fallen a couple of times during his follow through. Ernie Groves had made a trip to the hill to spread some sand where the pitchers were completing their strides.

In the fourth Luther hit the first pitch for a bloop double into left center. One out later Stuart Reems brought the infielder home with a single up the middle. On the bench, Joel watched as the Burlington first sacker walked slowly to the dugout. His jaw was set firmly; his facial expression was one of near exhaustion. Joel turned his eyes away from his friend. It hurt him deep inside to see the man suffering.

Joel's eyes picked up Joe Codrington sitting at the far end of the bench. His cap was beside him, and the right-hander was nervously running his fingers through his deep black hair. When he glanced at Joel, he merely shook his head slowly.

Tom Wyant just kept rearing back and throwing good stuff at the Bainbridge hitters. He was tenaciously holding on to his one run lead. Through the sixth he had given up but three hits and one base on balls. No Bainbridge base runner had reached third base.

The bottom half of the sixth started out with high hopes. Barney Kerr singled between first and second, and when the Bainbridge right fielder fumbled the ball, Kerr raced into second base. With Miller and Barber coming up, the Burlington fans were on their feet. Then Bainbridge drew the first break of the game. Chet Miller drove a hard line drive between short and third. The visiting shortstop reached across his body and speared the ball in the webbing of his glove. Kerr, at second, seeing the play made in front of him, stopped short and made his move back to the bag. In his haste, the Bears shortstop lost his footing and fell to his knees. The quick throw by the Bainbridge infielder doubled him off second. Luther came to the plate with no one on the bases.

Eldon Usher wanted no part of the Bears big infielder. With no one on base he simply pitched around Luther. His four pitches were nowhere near the strike zone. Reluctantly, the Bears power man moved down to first base. Meadowcroft ended the inning with a flyball into center field.

In the top of the seventh Bainbridge tied the game. Two singles and a long flyball put the visitors on the scoreboard. Wyant was still throwing hard, and George Hauser wanted to stay with his gifted right-hander. In the seventh he let Wyant hit for himself with a base runner on first. Wyant hit the ball hard, but the Bainbridge left fielder made a nice charging catch across his knees.

Wyant had an easy top of the eighth, but the Bears could do nothing in their half. Wilkins and Kerr grounded out, and Chet Miller got caught looking at a called third strike.

In the dugout, Joel found himself pacing back and forth, too nervous to keep his body on the wooden bench. Bainbridge was showing why they were league champions. Usher was still throwing hard, and the visitors defense had played flawless baseball. When their lead off man in the ninth singled sharply to left, George Hauser went to the mound. After a short conference with Wyant and Meadowcroft, the Bears skipper gave the pitcher a friendly slap on the back and returned to the dugout.

Breaks usually even up in baseball, and on the next pitch the Bears struck pay dirt. The batter bunted at the ball and looped a little short fly down the third base line. Miller grabbed the ball and fired quickly to first. The throw just nipped the base runner attempting to get back to the bag. With two down, Wyant took his windup and got the next batter on a high pop to Meadowcroft. As he left the field, Tom Wyant got a standing ovation from the Burlington fans.

Watching Luther Barber in the dugout, Joel suddenly felt the overwhelming feeling to say something to the husky batsman. Sliding down the wooden bench, Joel grabbed his friend by the arm. He could barely get the words out, but he did manage to say, "Wait on your pitch, Luther. He can't walk you this time. There's no way he's going to put the winning run on in the bottom of the ninth. I'll be pulling for you, Luther." Joel's voice cracked with emotion. Luther nodded, then pulled his big bat from the rack.

The Burlington fans were again on their feet, and the stadium seemed to shake with the sound of stomping feet and roaring voices.

Luther, beside the plate, took off his cap and wiped the perspiration from his brow. He then pulled the cap down tight on his head and stepped into the box.

Usher took his sign and swung into a long windup. The pitch was a breaking ball that dipped over the outside corner for a called strike. After taking some time, the Bainbridge right-hander leaned forward to start his motion. The delivery was another curveball that just missed the outside corner at the knees. Luther had been tempted but had held off at the last second.

As Usher took more time, the Burlington fans increased their noise in the stands.

The next pitch to Luther was another curveball that hung inside for ball two. The Bainbridge catcher gunned the ball back to his pitcher, and shouted out something behind his mask. Luther never moved from the batter's box.

Joe Codrington was standing at the third base end of the dugout. His hands were crammed into his back pockets of his uniform. His eyes were turned toward the outfield and the flag atop the center field pole. The wind was still blowing straight in from the bleacher seats. Joel walked nervously down to where the veteran pitcher was standing. Codrington's voice was strained and faint. "Here we are praying for a home run and we've hardly been able to get the ball out of the infield on this guy. It's hopeless, Joey."

BB

Getting his sign, Usher broke another breaking pitch across the outside corner. Luther started, and then held up on the pitch. The next delivery was a high fastball under Luther's chin. The string was out at 3-2.

Usher rubbed up a new baseball and stared down for his sign. He then took a smooth windup and brought a curveball spinning toward the plate. Luther took a long stride into the pitch and brought his bat around. The ball cracked off the dark piece of wood like lightning on a black sky. Joel jumped from the dugout to watch the flight of the baseball. Both the left fielder and the center fielder for Bainbridge raced toward the fence. To Joel it seemed like the ball was slowly being pulled down into the playing field. He kept repeating out loud, "Please get out of here!" "Please get out of here!"

The left fielder was at the fence looking up. Then the ball disappeared over the barrier. As Luther neared second base, the clouds broke and a beautiful ray of sun light streamed down upon the infield. Joe Codrington was running back and forth outside the third base foul line. He grabbed Luther half way between third and home and escorted him down to the plate. Within seconds the entire infield was filled with Burlington fans.

It seemed that the whole season had been played in just one ball game.

When Joel finally reached Luther, the big man was seated in the dugout. For a few fleeting seconds life had been a beautiful and perfect thing. The Bears infielder was crying and laughing with absolutely no embarrassment. When Joel squeezed his hand, he pulled the young pitcher's head down a little and said quietly, "I hit it good, Joey, but didn't you think it got a little push from somebody else?"

CHAPTER

15

PLANS FOR LUTHER

Timidity is a natural trait for a great many people, except maybe door to door salesmen and actors; however, there was nothing timid about the way Luther finished off Bainbridge in the remaining playoff games. In the fourth and fifth games at Burlington he struck doubles in the late innings to make the Bears 6-3 and 5-2 winners. In the sixth game at Bainbridge it was a Barber home run in the seventh with two mates aboard that gave Burlington the series four games to two.

While the Bears had been eliminating Bainbridge, Teal City had ended the season for Pottstown by taking four of the first five games. In the final best of seven series it would be the regular season second place finisher against the third place Burlington ball club. The first two games would be played at Teal City, followed by the next three at Burlington, unless one club swept the first four. If a sixth or seventh game was necessary it would be played at Teal City.

Joel lost the first game 2-1, but the Bears came back to grab the second game when Chet Miller homered in the top of the 13th inning. The third game would be an afternoon contest at Burlington.

On Sunday morning Joel walked the few blocks from his apartment to the big brick church on Wilmot Avenue. After services he stood for a few moments at the entrance of the beautiful house of worship. He was rather surprised when he noticed Luther Barber walking slowly from the church. Joining the older man, the two walked leisurely toward the middle of town.

"How does this great piece of architecture stack up against your church back home, Joel?" Then reconstructing his thoughts Luther stated, "That's an unfair question. What I meant to say was: How does the complete message of the church here stack up against the message back home?"

Joel pondered his teammate's question for a few moments. When he answered, he chose his words carefully. "I believe back home the church gives more careful and intelligent attention to the individual's inward needs. I guess it's a matter of bigness. Up here the membership is large; so are the offerings, but I think some have forgotten that whatever else may be religion's business, it most certainly includes the inward spiritual needs of each person."

Luther said nothing, but the powerful man with

the big shoulders hummed some type of old hymn through his closed lips. In the middle of the next block he said. "You know, Joel, my idea of a good minister or pastor is the type that a man wants to go to first when he finds himself in some sort of difficulty. Some just don't understand a man's problems, and certainly don't know what's going on among their own people. I figure there are plenty of people in this country who are eager for spiritual comfort, but they don't know where to turn. The shepherd has to understand the needs of his flock." After humming a few more bars of his hymn, Luther continued. "There was a minister back home in Oklahoma who was more concerned about folks playing baseball on Sunday than he was giving his congregation relief and advice. On the other hand, I knew another minister that had a lot of that quality which the old fashioned country parson had in such full amounts; the ability to give counsel lovingly and forgivingly."

Joel could not help but notice that Luther had lost some of the roughness in his speech since his early days on the club. His voice no longer held the bite and snap that it did when Joel first met his teammate in Florida. For a man who was thewed like a giant with the reach of a fighter and the eye of an eagle, Luther was mellowing just like Frank Knight said he might with time.

"Have you seen Olivia since the road trip?" asked Joel.

The sturdy infielder's eye brightened. "Saw her yesterday. I took some books and a Bears cap over to her about one o'clock. It was past three o'clock before I left the place." Luther smiled, "She's getting better by the day, Joey. Flashed the biggest smile I ever saw when I put that cap on her head."

Despite Luther's efforts to keep Olivia's home run under wraps, the word was out. Many of the Bears players had taken the time to visit Olivia. Many of the same players were very vocal in their appreciation concerning what the big first sacker had done for the girl.

126

After a few steps of silence Joel asked, "Luther, where will you be going when the playoffs are over?"

The big man's expression saddened a little. "I guess I'll be heading up the road to Virginia. Might try for a stevedore's job on the docks in Norfolk. Might be hiring this time of year."

The player's steps went onward. "You do plan to play baseball next season?"

"Can't say," came the reply.

"But you've had such a great season, Luther." Joel stopped for a moment to make his point." Forty four home runs, and just look at that runs batted in total. Nearly an average of one run batted in for every game played. Doesn't that mean anything to you?"

"It would mean a great deal more to a young man, Joey. I'm not going anywhere in professional baseball. I'm nearing the end of the road. This walking on and on into the dim distance with no goal at the end, would be bad enough at the best of times. A man needs to look forward, to see something he can strive for. For me, a man with a limited education, the opportunities are scarcer than thirty game winners in the big leagues." Pausing for a moment to remove his straw hat and wipe his brow, he then continued walking slowly up the walk. "Years ago I thought I might do some coaching in baseball when my playing days were over, but for the past few years I've stirred up so much trouble where I've played that no one cared about hiring me. George Hauser is the best man that I've ever played for in this game. He told me in spring training that this ball club was different than the others, and he knew what he was talking about. The players pull for each other, and when one player hurts, everybody hurts. I've never played with a bunch of players like that before. They've treated me fairly, Joey. I wish I could have played for Harley, George, and Frank when I was starting out. Things might have turned out differently."

The two players remained silent as they walked

past a portion of Burlington with its shops, its markets, its town hall, and its time worn church yards. Suddenly Joel heard his teammate say, "This is where I stay."

They had stopped in front of a small white house with a beautiful pathway of flowers leading up to its front entrance. To Joel it looked like a place where one could completely alienate himself from the bustle and sounds of the city.

"How in the world did you ever find this place, Luther?"

"To make a long story short, I was walking along this street looking for an apartment that was being advertised in the paper. This setting looked so attractive that I knocked at the front door and asked the lady if by chance she might have a room to rent. When I explained that I was a Burlington Bears player looking for housing, she showed me a pleasant room at the back of the house. Mrs. Howell is nearing 75 years of age, and has followed baseball in the city for a good many years."

Before Luther turned to walk up the narrow pathway, he asked, "Still reading all of those good books?"

"When I find time," answered Joel. "How about yourself?"

"Well, let's see now. At present I'm reading a little poetry. After I lost my wife, I started to read Burns, Keats, and Dryden. For some reason, poetry made me feel better, took my mind off my troubles. I bought a book that held a collection of English poems and another entitled Classic Myths. I sort of like mythology, too."

Joel was taken aback a little by Luther's comments. "Appears to me the public library has succeeded in giving you a pretty good literary education."

Luther laughed heartily. "I enjoy reading about men like John Keats. You know, Keats spent many of his early years in a place called Hampstead Heath, a pleasant area just outside London. Byron and Shelley used to visit him there. They say it's the most beautiful area in all of England. In fact, Crabbe, Wordsworth, Samuel Rogers, Coleridge, Campbell, and Joanna Baillie are only a few of the great literary people who have resided at Hampstead Heath. Can you imagine the history within that 240 acre area, Joey?"

The young pitcher threw up his hands. "Luther, you're talking in an area far over my head. I'm going to have to brush up on my English literature before discussing such matters with you."

Again Luther laughed loudly, "Brush up, Joey, but you had best hurry. We'll soon be going in opposite directions, you know."

When Joel dropped his head slightly, the big man was quick to change the mood. "See you at the park, Joey. I've got this feeling that you're going to pitch the best game of the playoffs. Don't be concerned about hitting support. I feel like belting a couple over that 380 mark this afternoon."

Joel took his time getting to the ball park. He couldn't get Luther off his mind. The man belonged in baseball; he belonged because he had so much to offer. Working on a dock in Virginia might be all right in the off season, but there was only one place for Luther seven months of the year, and that was on a baseball field.

Just as Joel reached the ball park, he felt some rain drops on his bare arms. And then the wind came. At first it came in little bursts, driving the rain against the brightly covered seats in the stands, but gradually it became steady, and at last it blew with uninterrupted intensity.

By game time the skies had opened up like a punctured water balloon. Thirty minutes later the game was called. It was rescheduled for the following evening.

The rainout gave Joel an opportunity to talk with Harley Walsh. He found his old friend sitting behind his desk, puffing on a stubby pipe, gazing out a window at the scattered puddles on the playing field.

When he noticed the pitcher, he gave a sweeping motion with his free hand. "Come in, Joey. Come in and have a seat. Something on your mind?"

Once settled, Joel struggled to find the best words to express his thoughts. "Mr. Walsh, I'm not sure I belong in here discussing this matter with you, but this business concerns Luther Barber, and I'm sort of worried about him. He says he might not be in baseball next year; instead he keeps talking about working on the docks up in Norfolk, Virginia. He thinks nobody wants or needs him in baseball, but I don't see how baseball can lose men like Luther. I guess he made a lot of mistakes with his life before he came here, but all the players on your club look up to Luther. He's straightened himself out and —

"Whoa there, Joey! Pull up for a second! What's the big question you're getting around to? Let me have it!"

Joel caught his breath. "What I was wondering about, Mr. Walsh, was your plans for Luther. I don't know if he would return for another season or not, but you are going to offer him another contract, aren't you?"

The owner took a long draw on his pipe and blew a puffy cloud of smoke toward the ceiling. When he spoke, his voice was low, like he was afraid someone outside the room would hear. "Joey, can you keep a secret?" After receiving a positive nod from the young hurler, the owner said, "Good. Now I'm going to let you in on a little something that's strictly confidential. As soon as the playoffs are over, I'm going to offer Luther a special contract for next season. I'm going to raise his salary substantially, and I'm going to ask him about joining the club as a player-coach! Frank wants to retire, and George will be needing a full time coach come next March. Think Luther might be interested?"

Joel grinned widely, "You can bet on it, Mr. Walsh. He thinks George Hauser might be the best manager in baseball. I've never seen two people get along better together than those two."

"Well," replied Harley, "let's leave this matter just the way it stands. I'll sit down with Luther in a few days and see what he has to say. Till then you're in the dark about all of this."

When Joel stepped from the small office, the sun burst through a break in the fast moving gray clouds. It happened just like it did when Luther hit his home run for Olivia.

CHAPTER
16
BOLT FROM A BAT

On Monday morning, after a brief lull, the late summer storm gathered and went howling into Burlington. Joel had eaten breakfast out and was nearly back to the apartment when the skies opened up. Now, just inside the side door, he watched the rain drip from his jacket, making small damp spots on the brightly colored rag rug at his feet.

It was late Tuesday morning before the sun peeped through, and the dark gray clouds moved away to the east. The two day rain was a blessing for Joel's tired right arm. If the game had been played on Sunday he would have had to throw with a mere three days rest. He had pitched with limited rest in the past, but his fastball always lost its zip in the late innings. Now, with Monday's game washed out, he would be pitching with a full five days of inactivity. His fastball would have plenty of life. If he could keep his pitches in the strike zone, there was no reason why he shouldn't have an outstanding game against Teal City.

Warming up in the bullpen, Joel cut loose with a number of high riding fastballs. Ed Wickland nodded his approval as the baseball popped loudly into his big mitt. Five minutes before game time, Joel picked up his jacket and walked to the dugout. George Hauser was at home plate with the Teal City manager and the crew of umpires.

Catcher Hal Meadowcroft stood on the front step of the dugout. After pulling on his mask, the chunky receiver stepped down to the bench and found a seat beside his young battery mate. Chet Miller walked by saying something about the bad condition of the infield. His voice passed, slowly receding. With feverish haste Meadowcroft started to talk. "Ed says you've got that good velocity, riding fastball tonight. Let's see if those guys can handle that kind of stuff. We'll mix in a good blend of breaking balls and straight changes. Their hitters barely touched anything you served up last Thursday. Tonight we're going to put you on top early with some instant runs." Before Joel could say anything, a roar went up from the stands and George Hauser was on his way back to the dugout.

In the top of the first inning Meadowcroft kept calling for the fastball, and Joel had no reason to shake the big catcher off. The first two hitters were late with their bats and went down swinging. The number three hitter popped a fastball up in the infield, and Barney Kerr gathered the ball in near the mound.

In the dugout, Meadowcroft had a few more words for his teammate. "Joey, I've probably caught you in thirty or forty games since you came to the club. You've always had a good fastball, but nothing like the one you're throwing tonight. Let's just keep using smoke most of the time until they prove they can get around on that kind of speed. For now the curveball is our second pitch. We'll sneak it at them when they're looking for the high, hard one."

Joel could not remember when he had registered so many early strikeouts. Through the fourth inning he had set down nine Teal City hitters on strikes.

In the bottom of the fourth Meadowcroft lined a triple off the fence in deep right center field. Jack Goodman then grounded a single between short and third to give Burlington a 1-0 lead.

There was no doubt that Bainbridge had been the best early and mid-season club in the Atlantic League, but in the fifth and sixth innings Burlington showed why they were the best late season club in the league. In the fifth Chet Miller made a diving stop of a wicked ground ball and retired the runner at first on a strong throw. In the sixth Eddie Wilkins went in back of second to make a great play and turn what should have been a base hit into a double play. In the bottom of the sixth Burlington added to their lead when Luther Barber caught hold of a high fastball and drove it far over the center field fence. Stuart Reems followed with another blast over the barrier in right center, and the Bears had a 3-0 advantage.

Joel gave up his first hit in the top of the seventh when the Teal City shortstop grounded a ball just out of Barney Kerr's grasp. With one out the next hitter looped a base hit into short right, sending the runner at first around to third. Joel took a deep breath and faced a big right-hand hitter who stood deep in the batter's box. Hal Meadowcroft flashed the fastball sign and moved his glove to the inside of the plate. Joel fired at the target, but the pitch was well out over the strike zone when the hitter made contact. The ball was lined directly back to the mound. Joel saw only a white blur of horsehide, then darkness. When he came to, he was lying on his back in front of the mound. His head hurt, and he could barely make out the faces leaning over him. Luther's voice burst through the grayness. "Take it easy, Joey. You've been struck by a batted ball. You're going to be all right. We're going to carry you into the clubhouse. Just take it easy." He could feel himself being lifted by strong hands.

133

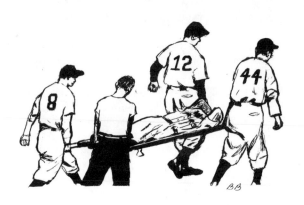

In the trainer's room his vision cleared a little. A doctor was checking his eyes and asking him questions. After nearly ten minutes of lying perfectly still, he was placed on a stretcher and removed from the small room. At the hospital the word was observation. It seemed to Joel that someone was always asking him questions and checking his condition. He felt tired, and his head thumped with pain, especially above his left eye. He was in the midst of answering another question when he fell off to sleep.

2

At the stadium the ball game moved into the ninth inning. In the seventh Teal City had tied the score. One run had scored on the drive which had injured Joel. Zoltowski had relieved with base runners on first and second, with one out. He managed to retire the next hitter on a fly ball to Goodman, but the next batsman had blistered a line drive up the gap in left center scoring both base runners. The inning had ended with a routine ground ball to Wilkins.

In the top of the ninth Zoltowski got the lead man on strikes and retired the next two batters on easy fly balls to the outfield. The Burlington fans were all on their feet as Jack Goodman led off the bottom of the

134

ninth. The Bears center fielder drove a fastball hard into right center, but Teal City's fleet footed middle outfielder made a nice catch near the fence. McCoy bounced out, and Wilkins grounded out weakly to second.

Carl Zoltowski was past his usual two or three innings of work, but his pitches were still popping into Meadowcroft's mitt, and he was snapping off a good breaking curveball to Teal City's right hand hitters. In the top of the tenth he retired the opposition in order.

In the Bears' dugout the players kept requesting information regarding Joel's condition.

Harley Walsh could only pass along what he had learned earlier. The young pitcher was resting, and was being watched closely. There simply was nothing else to report.

Barney Kerr led off the bottom half of the tenth with a looping single into short right center. Chet Miller tried to move the short stop along with a sacrifice, but popped the bunt up near the first base foul line. Luther Barber tossed a couple of bats away and headed for the plate. If Miller had succeeded in moving Kerr along with a bunt, Luther would probably have been passed, but now the Teal City manager was not about to walk the first baseman and move Kerr into scoring position.

The first delivery to Luther was a fastball under his chin which sent the slugger down in the dirt. Instead of backing off the plate, Luther set his feet a little closer to the inside corner of the base.

The next pitch was a curveball which started at Luther and then broke down and out toward the outside corner. The muscular hitter took a short stride toward right center and lashed the ball on a line over the second baseman's head. The center and right fielder for Teal City ran frantically to head the drive off, but the ball shot past both outfielders and headed for the barrier in deep right center field. Barney Kerr was gaining speed as he hit the bag at second and headed for third. Frank Knight's left arm was waving and turning like a windmill in the third base coaching box. Kerr made a perfect turn at the bag and raced for home. The relay from short right field was right on the money to the Teal City catcher, but Kerr did a fade away slide his left shoe just picking up the corner of the plate. "He's safe!" shouted the umpire.

Great offensive base running, and outstanding defensive work had produced one of the most exciting plays of the season. Burlington was now but two games away from the playoff championship.

Early Wednesday morning Joel opened his eyes and within seconds realized that his vision was greatly improved. The earlier throbs of pain above his left eye had receded. He heard a cheerful voice near the doorway of the room.

"Well, young man. How do you feel this morning?" The middle aged lady, dressed in the usual nurse's uniform, was carrying a small tray containing a glass of water and some sort of medication.

"I'm feeling much better," replied Joel.

"You had a very close call indeed. Apparently you managed to get your glove up a bit in front of that baseball. Slowed the force of the blow a little. Land sakes we can praise the Lord you were gifted with such quick reactions." The nurse walked to the head of Joel's bed and whispered softly. "There are a number of your teammates out in the waiting room. Feel up to a little visiting?"

Joel nodded his head slowly.

Luther Barber was the first Burlington player through the doorway. Barney Kerr and Eddie Wilkins were only a few steps behind.

"How you feeling, partner? We could have been in here earlier, but they padlocked your door. Mercy, what a scare you gave us. Joe Codrington fainted dead away. He's having his wife come up to see you this afternoon. Poor old Joe can't stand much of this stuff." Luther stopped his talking for a moment to grab a chair and seat himself near the head of the bed. "We won the game, Joey. I got lucky and mashed one into right center. Old Barney here was on first and took off like a spooked rabbit. His feet never touched ground between third and home. We won it in the bottom of the tenth."

Joey could not help but smile. The big man as usual was more than generous with his praise for other Burlington players.

"We're going to wrap it up in these next two games, Joey." Wilkins moved to the side of the bed. "Tom Wyant has the mound tonight and he says there's no way we're going back to Teal City."

Fifteen minutes later the room was again quiet, and a rather young looking doctor was standing over the young hurler. His voice was light and friendly. "Young man, you're going to be fine. For the time being, however, we're going to keep you in bed. If everything keeps looking up, you should be out of here tomorrow afternoon. For now, just relax and keep your movements to a minimum."

Joel had visits from several other Burlington players during the course of the early afternoon. Shortly before four o'clock he heard the sharp clicks of a lady's high heeled shoes in the corridor. Through the doorway to his room came a girl in a plain blue suit. One's first glimpse gave an impression of tailored finish and style. Her close fitting little hat owed much of its beauty to the face beneath it. Her eyes were soft blue, and beautiful brown hair shone beneath her pink straw head piece.

BB

"Joel, I'm Barbara Codrington." Her voice was soft, smooth, and agreeable. "I'm afraid Joe would be rather useless in this environment. He asked me to pinch hit for him this afternoon. Do you feel like visiting for a few minutes?"

"I would enjoy that very much," came the reply.

For the next half hour the subject of conversation changed a great many times. Joel found Mrs. Codrington to be a most informative young lady. There was not the slightest doubt in Joel's mind; Joe Codrington was a most fortunate fellow.

CHAPTER

17

TRAINS FOR DIFFERENT PLACES

On Thursday evening Burlington won the Atlantic League playoffs with a come from behind victory. Luther Barber cracked a two run double in the ninth to give Burlington the playoff flag. Carl Zoltowski was the winning pitcher.

Friday afternoon Harley Walsh met with Luther in the office at Bears Stadium. The meeting lasted less than fifteen minutes, and Luther signed a player-coach contract for the 1949 season. The monthly salary was the highest that the first baseman had ever earned in baseball. Harley also put a clause in the contract stating that the powerful hitter was to receive a sizable bonus if he hit more than 30 home runs and drove across a hundred runs.

Luther, tall, broad shouldered, the embodiment of

energy, stood outside the stadium, hands in pockets, and stared out across the city of Burlington. Directly in front of the ball park the quiet streets quickly led to busy avenues which in turn led one to the hub of the city. To the west one could see the green hills in the distance, hills that melted off in every direction toward smaller hillocks. Luther thought he could see cattle moving on the velvet slopes — mere specks upon the green, rumpled carpet, they were so far away. He was pleased that he would be returning to such a beautiful area. And the people — he had absolutely no complaints about the people. Harley and George had told him early in the season about the Burlington fans. He could not remember a single instance when they had gotten on him for poor play. When he had failed at the plate, the voices would roll from the dugout area, "Forget it, big man! Get him next time!" Funny thing, next time he seemed to try a little harder, and something nice usually happened.

And his teammates. To a man they had treated him fairly and squarely. Earlier in the season they had put up with his questionable behavior. Later on when he straightened himself out, he could sense a great band of friendship growing between himself and the entire roster of players.

And the press. Like the players, they were always fair and above board with their comments and dealings. He had made some lasting associations with members of the local media.

He checked his watch and noted that Joel's train was scheduled to leave in twenty minutes. Joel Travis — he sure liked the young man. He thought about that moment Tuesday evening when the young pitcher had been struck with that vicious line drive. He had been holding the runner on first base when the ball came off the Teal City batter's bat. He had thought at first that the ball had struck Joey directly in the face. He remembered he had yelled, "Oh no!" His feet could not seem to move toward the mound. How he had managed to reach the middle of the diamond, he could not remember. The next few minutes had been the longest of his life. Finishing the game had been the toughest thing he had ever been asked to do in baseball. How he had ever managed to drive Kerr across with that double was something he would never understand. Like the home run he had hit for Olivia, maybe someone else helped him get the bat around.

As he neared the train station, Luther thought about the boy's future in baseball. Joel would most certainly move into AAA baseball next season. He had won 15 games despite the fact he had reported four weeks late for the season. Luther knew Harley Walsh would do everything within his power to advance Joey into higher classification baseball.

The Connersburg youngster was standing on the spacious wooden platform. Two worn suitcases were resting at his feet. When he spotted the older teammate he shouted, "Luther! Luther! Over here!" Luther quickened his step and threw up his right hand in greeting. When he arrived at the platform he grabbed the tall hurler's hand in a firm clasp. Joey's physical condition looked good, but there was considerable blackness around and above his left eye.

The sun blazed down on the placid scene. There was scarcely a breeze now. Luther removed his hat and wiped his brow.

"Have you had your meeting with Mr. Walsh?" Joel seemed anxious to receive the big man's reply.

"We've had the meeting and I've signed my 1949 contract. I'll be playing and coaching for Burlington next season. Couldn't think of a place I'd rather be partner."

Joel had trouble holding back his feelings. "That's just great Luther. The fans of Burlington are sure a lucky lot having a baseball man like yourself around for who knows how many years. Some duo, you and George Hauser. I sure wouldn't bet against Burlington copping the pennant next year!"

Luther laughed and draped his arm around his teammate's shoulder. "I can't guarantee a pennant, but we'll be right in the thick of things. Of course the biggest problem we'll have is trying to replace players like yourself. For the past two days we've had players catching trains for all parts of the country. Most of them will probably be playing elsewhere next season. We may have to bring Frank Knight out of retirement to beat those bushes out there again. I wouldn't be surprised to see Chet Miller, Eddie Wilkins, and Jack Goodman, playing in AAA next season. Of course I'm expecting you to show those AAA hitters what a good pitcher looks like. If any of those fellows up there give you a hard time, just let old Luther know."

"Are you going up to Norfolk, Luther?"

"Just for a few months, Joey. Harley wants me back here by the first of the year. There's plenty to do before we leave for Auburn and spring training. I have a few suggestions about securing some replacement players. I suppose all of us will sit down and throw around a number of names. I want to make sure that Frank Knight sits in on those meetings. I sure respect his judgment on ball players."

People were stepping up into the low slung passenger cars. Someone yelled, "All Aboard!" Luther helped Joel with one of his suitcases.

On the first step of the car, Joel turned to ask. "I'm going to see you again next year aren't I Luther?"

The big man's face brightened. "I've got a feeling some place down the road we'll have a meeting. I'll keep things in order around here. You work hard and show those fellows out on the coast what a small town lad can do. Don't forget to keep me posted on your progress." Then with a more serious tone he added, "And don't forget all the good times we had together on this club."

When the train pulled from the station, Joel took one last look at his newest and closest baseball friend. Luther, wearing his smoky gray suit, and holding his straw hat, looked very much like he had when Joel first met him in spring training. The clothes were the same, but the man had changed a great deal.

To Joey, the prize at the end of the rainbow was not the winning of the playoffs; rather it was the re-birth of Luther. As the passenger sounded its lonely whistle, he wondered if he would ever see the big man again.